CLAIMED

FOUR PRINCES - BOOK 2

AUTUMN GRAY

This is a work of fiction. Names, characters, businesses, places, events, locales, and incidents are either the products of the author's imagination or used in a fictitious manner. Any resemblance to actual persons, living or dead, or actual events is purely coincidental.

Cover Art: Covers That Entice

ASI

Asi tucked Tarrin into his crib, praying he'd stay asleep and innocent forever. His chubby red cheeks made her want to kiss him all the time. It was hard to think her baby was now nearly two months old. His blond fuzzy hair stuck straight up along his head but was super soft. She was the luckiest woman in the world to have four men who loved her and the easiest baby in the world. Or maybe it was the fact he had five parents to care for him and rock him to sleep at night.

Tarrin let out a yawn as Asi adjusted the crib railing and patted his hand before leaving. If she was lucky, he'd sleep through the night as he had done last night for the first time ever. She didn't mind his late-night feedings but they did leave her feeling exhausted in the morning. Plus the doctor had given her okay to resume sexy times with her men and she couldn't wait to do more than snuggle with them.

As she came out of the baby's room, Kevin gave her a sexy wink as he leaned against the wall in the hallway. His crooked smile sending her pulse into overdrive.

"All set?" he asked.

"For what?" She brushed her silver-white hair out of her eyes. Really needed to book some time to herself and get a haircut.

"Our date. Remember?" His smile faltered. "Did you forget?"

She shook her head. "No, no, just got distracted with Tarrin. Let me grab my coat." Another awesome thing about having four husbands was there was always live in babysitters. Two demons and two vampires: her men, her husbands. She was a witch who was still learning about her power. Her studies on magic had stopped through with her pregnancy and she hadn't picked them back up since. The big baddie, Lucas, who was the demon king set to rule the world had been annihilated. None of the other demons, according to her two demon lovers, had taken up his mantle.

Asi donned the heavy wool coat and buttoned up the front. Winter had come early this year and they'd have a white Christmas in a month.

"Don't forget your coat," Kevin said from the front door.

She glanced down at his stylish sued shoes. "Right. You don't need anything to stay warm. Why can't I have that ability, then I wouldn't have to bundle up so much." She let out a chuckle because she still thought of herself as human but her men didn't. To them, she was their wife, lover, friend, and witch. Mostly, though, she was getting used to the idea of having four husbands, her princes, and her son not to mention throwing magic into the mix. Maybe she'd approach the subject of studying again with Kevin over dinner. Even if Lucas was taken care of, that didn't mean that she should forgo her abilities completely. What if she needed them again for a future attack? She pushed her hands into her gloves hating that she wouldn't be able to touch Kevin's skin until they were inside.

Part of her felt guilty for leaving the other three guys at home with the baby. "So what about the others?"

"Hmmm?" Kevin asked opening the door for her and leading her out in the snow.

Snowflakes fluttered about, the cold air biting her skin. She should've grabbed a cap and scarf.

"I mean, we don't need all of them to stay and watch the baby."

"Oh no," he opened the car door for her, "we haven't had alone time since we were on the run from Lucas and his demon horde. I drew the straw to get dibs to take you out first. The others will just have to wait their turn."

Her stomach did flips at his words at the promise of quality time with each of them. Did that also mean that he would be the first one of the four to resume their husband-wife alone time in the bedroom as well? He climbed into the driver's seat and clasped her hand in his while he drove them into town. Snow covered the trees making it look like Christmas was already here. Many people had already put up the brightly-colored lights on their homes and yards. She loved this time of year. But a pang of hit her that this was her first Christmas without her grandmother. Without any family.

"Hey, you okay?" he asked sensing her mood.

She sniffed her nose. "Yeah, just about Grams and about how I've no family left."

"Don't think like that." He frowned, his dark eyes glistening. "You've got our son and me and the guys."

She leaned over and gave him a kiss on the cheek. "And I'm so happy that I do. But I guess I wish my happiness hadn't come from so much loss."

"I understand." He grasped her hand. Then turned onto the main highway, the streetlights highlighting the caramel colors in his dark hair. “Grief is never something any of us can get over quickly. There is not something that happens during the day or night that brings up the memory of my fiancée, Shari. I still have dreams of her coming down the aisle before I realized Lucas had given her his demon blood and turned her into an addict like most vampires who drink our blood. It gets easier, the pain less intense but it never goes away."

"But we have each other and Tarrin, our son, and—"

"And the other guys." He gave her a sly smile that made her heart turn into triple beats. "Except sometimes I like having you all to myself like now."

"If I didn't know any better, I'd say you might have tweaked the lottery you four did." She snuggled up closer to him as he drove.

"Never," he huffed like he was offended. "I'm a demon not a monster."

She laughed, giving him another peek on his cheek. His temperature was always warm no matter the weather outside. But she already missed her son and what were the other three doing stuck at home without her?

When he pulled up to an Irish style pub, she slid out of the car and took his arm. "This is cool!"

"I hope you'd like it, wait to we get inside." He opened the door for her.

Heat and the scent of alcohol hit her. A soft rock song played in the background but the place was empty.

"Is it closed?" She bit her lip, sadness pressing down her chest.

"No," he whispered, sending shivers through her. "I bought the place out for the night."

"Wha—?" Before she could finish her question, Ralph, Simon and Ben stood up at a table at the back.

"Did you think we'd let you have your first night out since the baby and celebrate with only one of us?" Kevin asked.

"Actually, I did." She gave him a hug then rushed to the others. "But I like both ideas actually."

Ralph hugged her back and planted a kiss on her mouth. "The alone time is for later tonight and yes, Kevin did win this time but I'm next."

His promise sent desire spiking through her. But her new motherly instincts kicked in quieting her libido. "Who's watching Tarrin, then?"

"Jenna." Ben raked a hand through his dark blond hair. "Said we could stay out past midnight if we wanted."

Asi bit her lip, refusing the urge to check the time or call her friend and make sure everything was all right.

"What would you like to drink?" Simon bowed slightly. His coloring darker than his brother Ben's. Yet both men were vampires and stole her heart and breath every time she looked at them. "Irish whiskey or Guinness?"

She chuckled. "Neither, you know I can't have alcohol while I'm feeding Tarrin."

"Nope," Simon twisted his lips in a sideways grin, "I read up on this especially for tonight. As long as you pump and dump, should be fine."

"Or I'll help you out in that regard." Ralph rubbed his goatee, lingering his stare on her breasts which suddenly felt heavy under his gaze.

"Irish whiskey then, please." She took off her gloves and coat which Ben took from her and hung them over a bar stool.

The bartended nodded when Ben approached with an order of two Irish whiskeys and three Guinness.

"Care for a game?" Kevin gestured to a booth with a chess board sitting on the table.

"Sure." She squeezed into the cushioned bench with Simon and Ralph on either side of her.

Kevin sat across from her with Ben bringing their drinks and sitting next to him.

One sip of the whiskey and she let out a whistle. "God, that's strong but smooth. Almost like a bourbon."

"Don't let anyone hear you say that, love," Ralph whispered, tracing his hand up her thigh and sending her shivers of pleasure. "Irishmen get very testy with their drink."

"Your move." Kevin's wedding ring she'd given him tapped the side of his Guinness.

She frowned down at the board. It was really hard to concentrate with her men surrounding her and Ralph touching her. Then Simon rubbed his hand up her other thigh, making her squirm.

"Do you need more time?" Kevin cocked an eyebrow.

"Ye—no." All she wanted to do to was go home and check on Tarrin, then screw all her men one by one. Six weeks of no sex was eating her alive. Quickly, she moved her king-side pawn up two squares.

As if he had planned six moves ahead, Kevin moved out his queen-side knight. Asi took another gulp of whiskey. Both Ralph and Simon making her want to jump in their laps and let them have their way with her. And Ben stared at her like she was his favorite candy. Heat crept up her neck. She moved another pawn but she really wasn't into their game.

Two more moves and Asi finished her drink.

"I'll get you another." Ralph slid out of the booth and Ben took his place.

He placed his hand along the back of her neck, massaging the sore muscles there. "You're so tense."

No, I'm so horny. Is what she wanted to say. Instead, she moved another piece across the chess board.

"That move will cost you." Kevin winked, moving his queen to checkmate her. "An extra-long kiss."

Even though excitement buzzed along her body, she

still couldn't help wondering how everything was going with Tarrin. Must be new-mother jitters. Ralph returned with her drink and refill for the others as well. She downed the drink determined to enjoy her evening with her men and not let her fears and worries override her good time.

She leaned over the table and planted a kiss on Kevin's mouth that had her panting, wanting more. Reluctantly, she eased back. "Okay, what's next?"

"Dancing with me," Ralph standing beside the table held out his hand. "Then dinner with us. Simon's got a fancy dessert planned and Ben has another surprise."

"Can't wait." She took his hand pushing aside the unease that spread through her gut like a virus.

Ralph tapped a button on the old jukebox and a slow, jazz song came on. He pulled her to his dark chest, inhaling deeply. "You smell divine, Asi."

Her knees went weak but he held her up. She wanted him. All of them, now. But this was a public place and even though they'd bought it out for the night, the bartender and a waitress were still here and if they were having dinner and dessert here as well, then at least one cook in the back as well.

Midnight came too damn fast. Asi glanced at her watch after she took the last bite of chocolate mousse that she and Simon had made together in the pub's kitchen. Dinner had been nachos and French fries loaded with chili and cheese.

"It's getting late, I guess we should get back." She pressed a hand to her breasts as the heaviness of engorgement hit her.

"Ready to head home already?" Kevin smirked.

"Ah, yes, my boobs are killing me, and I can't give Tarrin some of this milk."

"That's okay, I'll take one side." Ralph smacked his lips.

"And I the other breast," Simon traced a hand across the hem of her jeans.

"Next time we go out, it'll be mine and Ben's turn to help empty your supply out." Kevin licked his lips.

She was turned on hotter than she ever thought she could be. "Let's go then."

The car ride home seemed to take forever and even kisses and fondles in the backseat didn't ease her growing nerves. When they pulled into the driveway, her heart screamed up her throat.

Fire licked the side of the house. The front door was blown off and laying two feet away in the snow.

"Tarrin!" She scrambled out of the car running full speed toward their home.

Inside the baby's room, the crib was empty. Black lines zigzagged along the walls. Grief stabbed her in the chest and she couldn't breathe. Her legs gave way but Ralph caught her.

"Our son, Tarrin, he's gone." Her voice was hoarse, the words burned her throat. "Where is he? God, where is my baby?"

RALPH

"What the hell happened?" Ralph pushed past both Simon and Ben who stood in Tarrin's doorway like statues.

The stench of sulfur filled the space and his heart plummeted at seeing the tell-tale signs of a demon ritual. Asi knelt in front of Tarrin's crib, sobs shaking her body.

Sorrow and anger clashed inside him making him want to break stuff, but instead he clenched his fists. "Where's the babysitter? Where's Jenna?"

Didn't matter if she was Asi's friend or not, if she participated in this, he'd rip out her spine.

Simon and Ben snapped to attention and fled the room. Despite the pain locking his chest, he moved to Asi, wrapping her in his arms. Her tears coating the front of his shirt.

"We'll find him." Somehow. Whoever did this knew exactly what they were doing. Ralph couldn't tell her that their son was now in hell being prepared for a sacrifice. The only luck they had was any infant ritual. It had to be a dark moon, which was two weeks away.

"Why Tarrin? He's a baby and innocent," Asi wailed. Her

face red as she glanced up at him like he was her hero and would fix this.

"I don't know," he lied. There was a list of demonic incantations that called for the blood of a baby—and theirs being born of four fathers and a witch—had very potent blood. Tarrin's life could bring forth a horde of demons from hell into this world. Or worse, resurrect Lucas, the demon lord they'd fought so hard to put down the first time. But who in the fuck would want to bring the bastard back?

Half the demons in hell were probably glad to see the tyrant gone. Another part was no doubt fighting right now to gain the rights as the new leader.

"We found Jenna." Simon's brow pinched. "She's in bad shape. Looks like she fought but a human is no match for a demon."

Shit. Was she dead then? Ralph couldn't ask in front of Asi. She was on the verge of a mental breakdown right now. "Okay, I'll see about her."

Reluctantly, he turned Asi over to Simon's arms. Ben nodded and he too wrapped Asi in his embrace. She stood in the middle of two strong vampires. They'd protect her with their life until the sun rose. In the meantime, Ralph needed to find out as much as he could before then. He didn't want the trail growing cold.

Even though there were two weeks until the dark moon, he didn't want to take any chances. Whoever or whatever had taken Tarrin had done so out of desperation. If it were him, he'd have waited until the night of the dark moon to strike. Take the child and do the death ritual at the same time. Or had the fiend that took their son believed that this was the only chance—with all of them away. Fuck! He never should've left a human to care for their son. Wasn't her fault, he needed to have stayed behind but he'd wanted to spend time with her like all of them had.

As he walked down the hallway, he fought the urge to punch into the wall. His insides burning with terror and misery. Felt like his heart was constantly shattering into countless pieces. He inhaled, his breath stabbing his breastbone as he marched into the living room.

Jenna lay on the floor unconscious but breathing. Part of her face and both arms bore the marks of a demonic Nasnas. Everywhere the creature had touched, was raw, opened flesh. She would need skin-grafts if she lived.

Carefully, he touched her shoulder. "Jenna? Can you hear me? We're getting you help but I need you to tell me what happened."

Kevin was on his cell phone in the kitchen calling an ambulance for her.

The stench of sulfur and cooked flesh assaulted Ralph's nostrils but Jenna didn't respond. Even if it was a Nasnas who attacked her, there were thousands of them in hell, and he doubted it was working alone. He needed more information to hunt down who took Tarrin.

"Please, Jenna, can you tell me anything? Was the demon tall or short, fat or thin? Did it have red or black eyes?" he asked, his desperation making the ball of emotion in his throat grow.

"The ambulance will be here in fifteen minutes." Kevin, his fellow demon, knelt on the other side of Jenna. "I don't think we'll be able to get any information out of her until her wounds are tended and she's on pain meds."

Which would make her sleepy. Ralph ground his back teeth to keep from bellowing. This was his family. The only one after his human parents discovered he was a half-Changeling and half-demon. Their previous pride in their perfect soon was swallowed by fear and loathing as they cooked him in holy water. The scars never had healed completely from his back, upper arms and legs. Yet, Asi and the others accepted him. They'd even tried a witch doctor to cure him, clinging to their ancestral roots, when the Catholics couldn't exorcize the demon out of him. That guy had taken the last of their money and left them with the false hope that forcing goat blood down Ralph's throat every morning would cure him.

In the end, Ralph had fled and never looked back. It was clear they'd wanted the son they thought they had and not him. His years of being the dutiful son and living with them for sixteen years had meant nothing when they discovered the truth.

He wanted to see the light burning bright in Asi's eyes again. Her happiness and love meant more to him than breathing. His nails bit into his palms. He had to make this right. Had to get their son back no matter the cost.

The ambulance pulled into their driveway. Red and blue lights throbbing against the snow in a hypnotic pattern. Ralph shook his head, pushing up from Jenna and opening the door for the paramedics.

They rushed inside and stopped short at her body.

"A Nasnas." He swallowed against the bile in his throat at the thought of what might have happened if Asi had stayed behind. True, she was a witch and not a mere human, but she was new to her power. What if the creature had overpowered her? She wouldn't have stopped fighting until it killed her. And from Jenna's wounds, it was clear she'd tried to do the same. She must have passed out from the torturous pain.

The paramedics both nodded, looking around nervously, then wrapping Jenna's wounds in special gauze reserved for burn victims. She'd always have scars.

Once the paramedics loaded her into the ambulance, Ralph spun on his heel and headed to Tarrin's bedroom.

He went past Asi and the others holding each other and ignored her soft sobs. Every fiber of his being wanted to comfort her but he had to figure out some clue to narrow down the millions of demons in hell that might have done this.

"What are you doing?" Ben frowned at him. His golden blond hair made him appear more like Asi's cousin than her lover or boyfriend. Not that Ralph's tawny skin would give anyone that mistake off the bat.

"Can you use your vision to see the past and find out who did this?" Ralph asked.

The vampire shook his head. "No. I've tried several times now but it's all a black void and gives me a migraine each time."

Ralph nodded. He figured whoever had done this knew them, and that they each had special powers. His own, freezing time and making people instantly trust him, wouldn't reveal the culprit either.

Asking Asi to use her power would be a mistake. With the state of despair she was in, who knew what might happen. She could end up blowing them up.

"All right, I've got to do a ritual then."

"Is that wise?" Simon stood, his arms crossing.

"Let him do whatever he can to bring Tarrin back." Asi squared her shoulders but her grey eyes were rimmed red.

It wasn't going to be a simple spell drawing a circle or pentagram and hoping for the best. This identifying spell could whiplash against him, trading his soul for the perpetrator's. But he couldn't wait days for Jenna to recover—if she ever did. Surprise and attack was their best option.

Kevin stood in the doorway, shaking his head. "If you're about to do what I think you are, then I'm in."

"No." Ralph couldn't let Asi lose any others in her life. "Stay with Asi and the others. In the meantime, take her and get yourselves to safety."

"I'm not leaving." She poked her finger into his chest.

"It's safer if you go. All of you."

She lifted her chin in a clear show of stubbornness. "Not a chance. I'm staying here so I have your back. We're a family, and we don't leave each other no matter the danger."

How could he make her understand? This wasn't a simple spell. If he lost her, his world, his heart, his very breath would be gone. "What I'm about to do is dangerous, Asi. I-I can't lose you."

She flattened her hand against his chest, her face determined. "You won't."

He wished he could believe her but every instinct inside him said her participating would be a terrible mistake.

KEVIN

"What do we need for the ritual?" Ben asked, holding onto Asi's hand while his brother, Simon, held her other one.

Kevin shook his head. Five years ago, he would have never imagined he'd be friends with two vampires or sharing his wife with them. Their wife. Asi was both witch and woman and his reason for living now. Before, he'd dedicated his heart and soul to bringing Lucas to justice and killing the bastard for what he did to Shari.

A snap of a twig sounded outside their home toward the backyard.

"Hang on a second," Kevin held up his hand, his senses on overdrive. "I think like someone's outside."

Ralph vanished in a flash, using his demonic teleporting ability.

"Guard her," Kevin demanded. After losing Tarrin tonight, he didn't want to take anything for granted. Guilt wore at his insides. He should have stayed behind to protect his son. Never should've suggested Jenna babysit. Now the memory sat like a mountain in his stomach. The human had been begging Asi and them for weeks to be able to watch the baby and the first time they agreed, look what happened? She'd nearly died—and still might—and their son. Their precious, innocent child was taken by a fucking demon. He clenched his teeth so hard he was sure they'd crack.

Kevin teleported outside near where he'd heard the noise. For a moment, he didn't even breathe. Searching the area for any other sounds. Nothing. Clouds hid the moon while a cool breeze stirred up fallen leaves. Someone or something had been right here.

He closed his eyes, focusing his main power of being able to hear better than any animal or being alive, for any other sounds that didn't belong.

An owl hooted a half-mile away. Two bats zipped overhead but no more crunching leaves or twigs sounded. Whispers of Ben and Simon consoling Asi from inside the house reached him but nothing that wasn't supposed to be out here. Ralph opened his eyes. But something had made a noise too close to their home and it wasn't random or an animal. He was certain of it. He felt it in the core of his being that whatever had been here had teleported out like them—which meant another demon. Grunting under his breath, he mumbled a curse. He should have caught the creature before and they wouldn't be in this situation. He'd have happily ripped it apart.

"Anything?" Ralph walked toward him.

He shook his head, his instincts telling him to be wary and not assume he'd heard wrong. "No, nothing. But there was someone here."

"I believe you," Ralph said. His dark skin blending in with the night not that he needed any help sneaking up on someone. "I'll do another sweep of the area, go and help Asi. See if you can convince her not to participate in the demon location ritual. You of all people know how dangerous it is."

Indeed. It was worse than doing both Ouija Board and séance and painting a bulls' eye on their chest for any lower-level demon that wanted to possess someone to come and try. Hell, with Asi's magic, they could lure in a big baddie pretty easily.

"Call if you need me," Kevin said, then hiked up to the house. Leave it to Ralph to make him the carrier of bad news. He had nothing against the half-demon/half-fae but last time he had to do something like this he and Simon entered a hellish shit storm. He had taken Simon with him to Lucas' lair to retrieve a magic book, both he and the vampire had been captured. Even Ralph had his doubts about Kevin's loyalty because the spell book hadn't been there. Almost like Lucas knew they were coming and nearly succeeded in breaking up their group.

But each of them was loyal to Asi. How could their plan about the book have been discovered? That question had plagued him since he and Simon had entered the library to find the book in its glass security case, gone. It had been Ralph's idea for them to go and retrieve it for Asi. Had he double-crossed them? Why? And was him sending in Kevin to the house so he could meet up with whoever had been out here?

Stop it! Kevin push away the doubts snaking in his mind. Out of all of them, Ralph was the one who brought them together to help Asi when her grandmother died. Unless he wanted Asi for himself and had planned for Lucas to kill two of them in hell but they'd escaped.

Kevin shook his head. No. He had come to save them. With Asi. So had he needed to save face by showing her he wasn't responsible for their capture?

Unanswered questions swirled in his mind as Kevin entered the house and the demonic stench of sulfur and blood hit him again. They'd need to do a house cleansing and a blessing whenever Ralph finished with the demon location spell. For now, they had to leave as much of the goo here to use to find the devil who did this.

When he walked into the bedroom, both Simon and Ben tensed before relaxing at seeing him.

"Where's Ralph?" Asi asked, her eyes swollen from tears.

"Double-checking the area but found nothing in the first sweep. Probably just a deer passing through." He lied, not wanting to worry her any more than she already was.

"Thanks." She took a shuddering breath and placed her hands on Tarrin's crib. "What do we need to do to get ready for this ritual?"

"Asi, I really don't think it's a good idea for you to participate." He stopped when she gave him a death glare. "It's dangerous. Maybe more than when we faced Lucas. The ritual will call up demons—some of which hunt for humans to possess—if they took over you or one of us, I don't know what would happen."

"But with all of us and using my magic, the ceremony will be stronger." She cocked her head to the side. "We'll take precautions but I will not leave finding my son to chance."

"I'm not asking you to do that, either." He took a step toward her and Ben and Simon giving them space. Giving them a nod of thanks, he rubbed Asi's back. "But we need to be safe and that means following mine and Ralph's directions no matter what."

She leaned against him, pressing her back to his chest and bringing his arms around her. "I'll do whatever it takes to get Tarrin back even if that means taking down all the demons in hell."

His heart froze, believing she'd do just that. Even if it meant putting herself in danger.

ASI

"What do we need for the ritual?" Asi asked turning from Kevin's hold. "It'll be daylight in a few hours and I want Simon and Ben involved."

"Are you rushing this a bit?" Simon frowned. "I mean you're still human and you've not slept since last night."

"And I won't get much sleep with Tarrin gone." She rubbed her arms. "Not until he's found and brought back home. Safe."

"The ritual will use all of our powers." Kevin moved to the baby's doorway. "I'll be back with supplies. In the meantime, clean up Tarrin's things so it's only his crib in the middle of the room and nothing else."

"What about the black goo on the wall?" Ben pointed his chin to the ectoplasmic residue.

"Leave it. We'll need that to pinpoint the demon who did this," Kevin said and disappeared out of the room. His heavy footsteps echoed down the hallway to the kitchen.

Asi bent and picked up the stuffed teddy bear she'd bought for Tarrin last week. She clutched it to her breasts, her sobs hammering against her chest. Her son. Her baby!

Fresh tears pricked her eyes but she shook her head as Ben approached her. It wouldn't do Tarrin or her or anyone any good if she crumbled in a heap and cried.

Moving as though she pushed through quicksand, she picked up a few more toys, dumping them onto her bed in the next room. She stared down at them, a hiccup cry strangled in her throat. Her heart, her soul, all of her felt hollow inside. Like someone had scooped her out and all she was, was a shell walking around. How could she live without her baby? Never hearing his cry or seeing his smile. He was so young and innocent—what if they never found him—Simon!

He had the gift of seeing the future. Multiple ones as any deviation in the current time line would breed hundreds more paths. But it was something. She had to know if they had a chance to bring Tarrin back. Somehow.

With hope blossoming a tiny vine in her heart, Asi raced back to Tarrin's bedroom and crashed into Simon. "Quick! Use your power, please."

"Whoa, whoa, whoa." He held her a step away from him and brushed her hair out of her face. Concern filling his dark eyes. "What are you talking about?"

"I know you don't like to view the future that much, because it's so unpredictable, but could you...would you check on Tarrin? I have to know if at least one of your visions shows he's okay. That we get him back safe and sound."

When he hesitated, she gripped his shirt. He had to do this. Wasn't he as worried about Tarrin as she? If she had his power, she'd travel down every remote thread of the wheel of time until she found one that worked. One that brought their baby home.

"It's not that easy. Looking into the future is not only draining but doesn't reveal the truth. It could be one possibility out of millions. Billions even."

His words stung her. "Y-you won't even try?"

As she pulled her hands off his shirt, he placed his over hers, keeping her in place. "I didn't say that. But you might not like what I find and there are demons involved which screws the timelines up even more. If we were dealing with a human kidnapper then sure."

A tremble rocketed through her body at the word kidnappers. "Please, I have to know. Can you at least find out if he's okay?"

He pressed his forehead to hers. "I will try my best to find Tarrin and what will bring him back safely. Okay?"

"Fine." She let out a hiccup sigh, brushing her lips across his. "Thank you."

Ben stepped forward, his power reverse his brother's. Not only Simon's older brother but also his opposite image. Light hair, blue eyes that turned red when he needed blood. Even his power was the opposite of Simon's future readings, Ben could only see the past. Whoever had taken Tarrin also knew that. Knew that they'd have to work in the present quickly to keep both vampire brothers clueless until this tragedy happened. Asi stepped out of Simon's embrace and wrapped her hand in Ben's while they waited.

Last time she'd touched Ben when he wanted to show her what happened to her parents, the magic that sparked between them knocked both her and Ben on their ass. No, she had to be ready for the ritual and not end up locked in an endless sea of potential futures.

Simon sat down near the opposite wall from the black streaks of ooze. "Go ahead and keep clearing the room. You won't disturb me and I don't know how long this will take."

Not trusting her voice, Asi nodded letting go of Ben's hand so they could keep taking Tarrin's things out of his room. Somehow it felt wrong though. Her cleaning out his toys and clothes. Like he wasn't going to come back ever.

That they were clearing out his space and it would forever remain empty. She pressed her hand to her mouth, stifling sobs that welled up from deep inside her.

Ben hauled her into his arms, whispering, "It's okay, Love, we'll find him. Everything will work out and we'll have your spicy, jalapeño burgers and chocolate shakes with way too much syrup."

Her sniffles made her body shake as he held her. What would she do without her men? But now someone had her baby and should wouldn't let them get away with it. No, she might be a hysterical, crying mother now, but when she found out who had done this, she'd blast them into a bazillion pieces.

Kevin returned from the kitchen with matches, candles, and a box of salt tucked under his arm. After setting the stuff inside, he and Ben moved the crib into the middle of the room.

"Take the photos and pictures out too," Kevin pointed to the walls. "But nothing on the infected wall's side."

Again, an emptiness consumed Asi as she removed the letters over Tarrin's window that spelled his name. This felt so wrong but they had to figure out who had done this.

Satisfied when they were done, Kevin nodded, then paused. "Where's Ralph?"

"Last time I saw him, he went outside with you." Asi frowned. How had she missed him being gone all this time? It was Ralph who she first started falling for. Out of all of them, he was like the leader of their group. Always having a kind word, always able to make her feel better. And he had a gentle nature too—fixing her wounds after her and her grandmother's car crash. Back then, she'd never have thought a demon would care enough to study medicine to help people. She'd been wrong about so many things in the beginning.

The front door slammed shut and Asi's heart leapt into her throat. "Ralph?" she squeaked out.

"Smells like someone else." Kevin's words echoed in the silence.

"Stay here," Ben growled.

He and Kevin charged down the hallway to intercept whatever had just entered their house.

Stay? Like she was a child? No way! She gave a quick look at Simon still meditating, a trickle of sweat coursing down his cheek but she couldn't stop him from hunting through time. Not now or ever. She had to know about Tarrin. And she wasn't going to wait here for Ben and Kevin to confront whoever had dared enter her home uninvited.

She marched down the hallway and past the living room. But when she reached the foyer, she skidded to a stop. Her heart beating so hard she thought it would break her breastbone.

Ralph swayed on his feet, covered with black tar. It covered his entire body leaving only his eyes visible.

Both Kevin and Ben gawked at him but neither moved any closer than the two feet they were from him.

"What's that on you?" she asked, fear drumming in her chest. "Did you find the demon who took Tarrin?"

He shook his head. "No. This is what's left of a Nain Rouge."

"Which is what?" She looked from him to the other two.

"Many believe he's a red dwarf but he's more sinister than that," Kevin said. "He's a demon trickster and some say a harbinger of doom."

"We've got to get this stuff off him." Asi turned toward the half-bath to grab some towels. "Is it poisonous?"

"Only to humans." Kevin caught her elbow.

"Best if you don't get any of this toxin on you." Ralph smiled.

With a nod, she pulled away from Kevin and handed him and Ben an armful of damn towels.

"The wash won't clean these, we'll have to burn them later," Ralph said.

They moved to the kitchen where Kevin quickly spread out the Sunday newspaper they hadn't even gotten to read yet. Ralph moved to the center of the papers. All three of them wiped as much of the tar-like substance off Kevin, while she leaned against the kitchen counter.

Was the fact this Nain Rouge had been here meant that Tarrin was truly lost? She swallowed against her raw throat, the heartache inside her festering. "So did Ralph kill a harbinger of doom?"

Ralph wiped a towel over his face, then met her gaze. "The fucker always pops up before a catastrophic event. Humans have spotted him before the Battle of Bloody Run, the War of 1812, and even a horrible snowstorm in 1976 among many, many more."

Her stomach fell. "Why was he here?"

"To freak us out." Ben folded up his dirty towel and reached for another to wipe Ralph's back. "It's a demon, no offense guys, it's whole reason for being is to spread evil."

"There are many Nain Rouge in hell." Ralph rolled back his shoulders as if they were sore. "This one was probably sent to distract us or at the very least spy on us."

She straightened. "Then, did you find out who took Tarrin? Who was the Nain Rouge working for?"

"No idea. The bugger attacked me and exploded before I got a chance to ask." Ralph frowned. "Almost like it had been triggered with a kill-switch if it got too close to one of us. I'm just glad it was me and not you."

Despite her sorrow, Asi found herself giving him a soft

smile back. "Okay. Let's focus on the ritual then. Sunrise won't wait and I don't want the trail going cold."

"Give me twenty minutes to wash the rest of this stuff off." Ralph nodded. "But go ahead and get the circle ready."

While he went into the shower, Ben and Kevin threw the towels and newspapers into a metal wheelbarrow outside. Then they returned inside, washing their hands and arms up to their elbows in Ralph's medical-grade soap.

"I'll meet you in Tarring's room," Asi called over her shoulder. "Seen enough movies to know how to make a circle."

"Do the candles first, the salt is last." Kevin turned off the faucet.

Asi ducked into Tarrin's room and grabbed the candles and matches from the floor when it felt like someone was watching her. She spun, her free hand raised to blast whoever was in here. "Simon?"

Unmoving, his eyes stared at nothing. Blood ran rivets down his face like he was sweating blood.

"Oh my god, Simon!" She rushed to him, the candles and matches falling from her hands. Was he locked in one of the futures? If she touched him, she could get trapped too but she had to do something. "Help! Kevin, Ben!"

Kevin teleported beside her. "Asi, wha—stand back."

"What's wrong with him?" This was all her fault. If she hadn't insisted he try and find a future where Tarrin was returned to them...

A second later, Ben raced into the room with his vamp speed. "Fuck! Simon, snap out of it." He knelt in front of his brother, his hand shot out and grabbed Simon's chin, making him look at him. "Come back to us. The present."

Simon's lips moved but no sound came out.

"Use my magic too," Kevin sat in front of Simon and held out his hand.

Ben clasped his hand and kept his other on his brother. Behind them, Asi paced, guilt gnawing on fragments of her soul. *Please, please let him wake.* She repeated over and over again.

"It's not working," Ben said like he was exhausted.

Asi scooted closer. "Let me help. Use my magic too like you did with Kevin's."

Both men looked at her, then nodded.

When she took Kevin's hand, white lightning snaked out of each of them and into Simon. He screamed and she jerked away.

"Stop, stop, we're hurting him."

Simon gasped, coughing. "Give…me…a…moment."

Relief flooded her. He was okay. She leaned forward to touch his hand but he shook his head.

"No. I found out who took Tarrin and I don't want to lose the vision until I decipher it."

"What's there to interpret?" Asi asked, her heart swelling in her throat. "Who took him? Who took our son?"

His bloodstained eyes stared at her as if judging if she could handle the truth.

"Whatever it is, whoever it was, you can tell us." Asi grasped Kevin's hand. With everything she had, she willed Simon to tell them what he'd seen. Her patience wearing super thin as she fought the urge to yell for him to say who the vile kidnapper was.

"Lucas did this. Lucas has our son," Simon said in a hoarse voice.

She felt all the blood drain from her face. Her head felt heavy. "No, no that's not possible. He's destroyed…we killed him."

SIMON

"That can't happen, right?" Asi's face paled, her voice a raspy whisper. "He can't come back from the dead."

Simon wanted more than anything to tell her that he was mistaken. But in all of the futures he'd visited, Lucas had appeared in each one. His mocking, demonic laugh still ringing in Simon's ears.

How was it possible the demon lord could be in so many of their futures? They'd killed him. Simon had seen him die with his own eyes.

All of the futures now showed Lucas alive. Even using their son to increase his abilities and strength while they and the world were shackled in darkness. That image would kill Asi if she'd been in any of those visions. But even more disturbing was who else had appeared alongside Lucas.

"How is it that you saw Lucas alive and in the future?" His brother asked. "Did you cross into another reality somehow?"

Not impossible but difficult.

"I don't think so. He looked the same as he did before."

Simon's gut clenched. The demon lord looked healthy and fucking giddy even. Almost like he knew that Simon was searching and could see him. But again, that couldn't happen. Lucas was dead.

"Here." Asi handed him some wipes. "You've got blood on your face."

"Really?" That's hadn't happened before. Is the monster's blood what skewed his timelines in the future? Or the fact that he'd worked so hard to find a solution to who took Tarrin and how to get their son back?

He wiped his face, surprised when the toilette came back dark red.

"Why isn't the ritual circle ready?" Ralph asked from the doorway, his hair damp, wearing different clothes than earlier in the night and looking like he's been dragged half-way through a torture chamber.

"Did you find anything outside?" Simon asked.

"Just a demonic minion here to cause trouble." But a look of wariness passed over Ralph's face. "Let's get the ritual done before sunrise and Asi can get some rest."

Simon snorted, reading between the lines. What the demon meant was he and Kevin, being the only demons and not subject to things like sleep and the sun, would get a head start on tracking down those responsible for taking their son. Envy prickled across his skin. He wanted to be the one taking care of Asi morning, noon and night, but that was impossible for a vampire unless he wanted to end up a pile of sizzling ash.

"I'm going too." Asi picked up a candle and placed it around Tarrin's crib.

"No, you need to get some rest. Let me and Kevin handle this first part. Even if we get a reveal through the ritual, it could narrow down the suspects from several thousand to several hundred." Ralph grabbed another candle and set it several feet from hers.

"We promise to alert you as soon as we find out anything," Kevin added.

Asi huffed but desperation filled her eyes despite the dark rings underneath them. "I could do a spell that would help me go without sleep or food for days, then I could help you search."

Simon straightened. Messing around with anatomy like that was dangerous. Her own twin sister, Tara had tried something similar but the power she absorbed was too much and killed her. Even though she was Asi's sister, she was so different from her sibling. Asi hadn't cared about magic or power but Tara craved it like a junkie. He hadn't felt right about sharing his ability with her then she found her own vampire to grasp his power and it killed her and the other half of their circle they'd begun forming.

Asi's grandmother had wiped her memory of her sister from Asi's mind until Simon had revealed the truth three years later when Asi was twenty-one. But the idea of him and his brother being able to help in the search and not be comatose from sunrise until sunset was tempting.

Even though vampires, he and Ben be outside in daylight for a small amount of time in the early morning or late evening but it came with a price of blisters. Plus, it took damn longer to recover. But he would walk through the middle of the day, die for her, if it would bring Tarrin back. Whoever did this had to be hiding behind a mirage of Lucas. That was the only explanation because the demon lord was dead. Asi had tied a curse to his death as well that only someone who truly loved him would be able to save him. And the bastard had no one. His demon army would rally behind any leader. No one would be able to resurrect Lucas because love couldn't be faked.

Simon took Asi's hand in his leading her to the center of the room inside the circle around Tarrin's crib. "No matter what happens, know that I will never stop until we find our son."

She nodded, tears welling in her eyes.

Soon the other three men joined them with Ralph sealing up the magic with a ring of salt around the outside of the candles.

"Asi, would you light the candles please starting in the south," Ralph instructed.

Taking a breath, she went to the back of the circle. She pressed her hands toward the candles, whispering an incantation. Flames sputtered to life.

"Now the west," Ralph said.

"No, the east would be next wouldn't it?" Asi frowned looking from the west to the east side of the room.

"Normally, yes, but this isn't a regular ritual. We're having to do things backward to map into hell and find the bastard responsible." Ralph faced the west, waiting for her to light the candles in that location.

Asi squared her shoulders and her magic ignited the candles there. "Now the north than east, right?"

"Yes," Ralph said looking from her to Simon, then at Ben and Kevin. "As soon as you light the east, be ready."

"For what?" Simon took a step toward him.

"We each will need to hold the circle with Asi in the middle."

"Oh fuck!" Ben shook his head. "How are we supposed to do that?"

"As well as you can and as long as you can until I can weed out who might be responsible, then we go kick some ass." Ralph moved to the east corner of the circle.

"Is there a special direction we should take?" Ben asked.

"I'm a demon," Kevin said, "I'll take the south which is the element of fire."

Simon moved opposite of Kevin's side of the circle. "I've got north."

"Guess I'll take water." Ben shrugged.

"That makes sense," Simon smirked, "You always did want to be a merman when we were kids."

"Shut up!" Ben shot the finger at his brother.

Asi gave a little chuckle and Simon didn't care if Ben tried to beat his ass later. Seeing her smile a fraction was worth it.

Next, Asi lit the candles in the north then moved to the east where Ralph gave her an encouraging look.

As soon as the last of the candles were burning, the room shook. *Holy fucking shit!* Whatever was happening couldn't be good.

"Quick, Asi, to the crib," Ralph said. "The rest you, stay in your spots, focus your energy on keeping the circle intact."

Another quake shook so hard that Simon struggled to remain standing. A pressure built against his side of the room as though a giant fist pounded against them. Images and colors blurred out of his reach.

Tantalizing. He wanted to touch them. See if they were real or if he could get them to slow down. He raised his hand, fingers outstretching past the candles' flames.

"Simon," Ralph yelled. "Don't break the circle!"

He looked back at the others briefly but their expressions showed concern and worry not the bliss he was experiencing. Didn't the half-demon see the wonders beyond their enclosure? The sun glinting off the snow-topped mountains? Or the sunrise peeking across the ocean's waves?

If he could stretch a bit more, he'd be able to reach either of them. Find the warmth of a beach and bask in the sun. He wouldn't be burned, not in this place.

Muffled voices called his name but he was so close to the

beach. He hadn't felt the sun's rays or made a sand castle in forever. All he needed to do was move another inch and he could touch the sand.

A scream rent the air around him, shattering the illusion before him. *Asi!*

Simon spun around. Their circle was still in place but dark forms swam over Asi in the middle of the room beside the crib. She was two steps closer to him than she'd been when they started.

"I told you to hold your line in the circle," Ralph growled. "Look what you've done!"

"Shit!" Simon swallowed against his raw throat. "What do we do now?"

A bat-like creature swooped down, its talons slashing across Asi's back. She flinched, careening backward.

"No! Asi!" His heart stopped in his chest. He couldn't get to her. Not in time and not if they wanted to keep the circle intact. If he rushed to her, more hellish things would break through.

Why wasn't she using her magic to destroy them?

As though reading his mind, she raised her hands, her palms glowing.

"No! You can't use your magic in the circle," Ralph yelled. "It'll blow apart the circle."

"Then how the fuck do we get rid of these things?" Ben dodged one, his foot slipping and he almost toppled out of the circle.

"They're spiritual beings, not physical," Kevin grunted as two charged him. "You won't be able to affect them anyway no matter how much power you tossed at them."

One of the demonic things slashed its claws at Simon, catching him across his cheek. He punched the creature but his fist went through air. "Yet the buggers can attack us all they want. How do we get rid of them?"

"Stay in your spots, guard your part of the circle." Ralph pointed to Tarrin's crib. "Asi, get back to the center. Your element is spirit and it connects all of us."

Asi moved like she was in wet cement. In a sudden rush, more creatures rushed out of the portal and targeted her.

"Keep going!" Simon encouraged but cringed as each bat shrieked and dug their claws into her back, her arms, her legs.

She screamed in pain. Blood ran rivets down her clothes as she took one step. Her body trembling and Simon moved toward her. His heart felt like it was being crushed to see her injured.

"Stay where you are, Simon!" Kevin and Ralph beloved.

He slid back, clenching his fists as more and more of the spirit demons flooded Asi's small flame.

Soon, Asi's small frame collapsed just outside of the center of the circle.

"Fuck this!" Simon dashed forward, trying to knock the creatures off her. But the vial creatures turned and attacked him. They bit and clawed his hands.

Asi reached for him, pain etched in her face. Her trembling hand stretching for him. "Hurry," she whispered.

He pushed forward, brushing his fingertips against her palm. His power flooded from him into her.

"Get back!" Ben yelled.

Simon's attention snapped to the north end of the circle. Black ooze bubbled out of the carpet, chewing on everything in its path.

"Fuck!" Simon tucked Asi against him to protect her but her skin was cold like she'd been in a blizzard.

"Close the circle, quick." Ben skidded to a stop beside Asi and Simon, wrapping his arms around her too. "Fucking, close the circle!"

Ralph and Kevin scrambled to each of the elemental

quarters, closing each one until only the north remained. "We need all of us to do this one."

Helping Asi rise, Simon's heart slammed in his throat at the hollowness in her eyes. So she'd seen his visions. The ones that showed who was responsible for Tarrin's abduction.

She'd seen Lucas alive and well and standing beside him with a smirk, was herself.

ASI

It's not possible. It's not true. There was no way she would ever aid in bringing Lucas back much less giving him her son. Yet countless flashes of the future she gleaned from touching Simon, in each one, she stood side by side with their enemy. Tarrin's lifeless body at their feet.

Her insides felt as if she'd been hallowed out. An empty shell that would never be whole again. Never hold her son again and smell that newborn scent or feel him nuzzle her while she kissed his soft forehead.

Grief sank into her gut, strangling what little hope she had left.

"Asi." Simon brushed a tear from her cheek. "We need you to help close the portal."

"Why?" If all the futures that had flashed showed her son dead and her with Lucas, why would she want to continue? "Let them kill me now."

Then the visions wouldn't come true. Without her in the picture, maybe Lucas wouldn't be resurrected and her men could rescue their son.

Simon placed his hands on either side of her face, making

her look up to him. "I-I know what your vision showed because I saw it too. But there has to be some reason. Don't take a vision at face value until we know the facts. Right now, we've got to stop this demonic blob from crossing over into the real world. This thing could harm hundreds of people. Please, Asi, focus. Use your power with ours to shut the circle down."

"You can do this," Ben whispered next to her.

Across from them, Kevin and Ralph fought back the blob as best they could but it gained a centimeter every second.

Asi gathered up her rage, her magic, her hopelessness of her baby gone and shoved all of it into a magical sphere. The ball wobbled toward the goo chewing at the far end of the circle. When it struck the demonic oozing acid, the creature let out a shrill sound that pierced Asi's ears. She slapped her hands to shield herself from the noise, looking to her four men and seeing them doing the same. Kevin, though, was on the floor in a ball.

His was pale as he curled farther in on himself, his hands on his ears. Dark blood pooling from his nose and eyes.

"Kevin!" She rushed to his side.

The creature's keening cry never relenting.

She had to help him but she couldn't even think or focus her magic with the shrieking noise burning her eardrums. Taking her hands from her ears, she bit the inside of her cheek as her eardrums throbbed and a headache bloomed across her skull. Healing Kevin would have to wait until after she stopped this noise maker.

"Shut up!" she yelled, thrusting her hands forward. The magic ball ricocheted off the creature making it squeal even louder.

She crumbled to the floor unable to keep her hands from covering her ears. How would she fight it if she couldn't use her magic?

Ralph, Ben, and Simon gathered around her. Not needing words, their gazes told her to take their magic as well. Ralph placed his hands over her ears, then Ben followed, and Simon. Each giving her a buffer to concentrate and get rid of the monster.

Her hands trembled as she raised them, pointing them directly at the creature. Another magic sphere tingled from her core and out her arms and hands into the blob. This time, the thing shuddered, momentarily silencing its piercing wail. Seconds later the squeals vibrated from the creature again. Kevin on the floor now started to seize.

"We have to help him," Asi moved to go to him, her lungs constricting with terror.

"No! Fire at the blob. Again, again," Ralph shouted.

Quickly, she sent two more consecutive shots. Her legs buckled from the excursion and Ben moved his hands from her ears to help hold her up.

"It's not working." She shook her head. Panic swelling in her chest and she couldn't take a deep enough breath. Adrenaline surged through her. The urge to flee was overruling the urge to stay and fight but she'd be damned if she let some monstrous beast take her home.

"Focus on closing the circle," Ralph yelled. "Maybe you can close it on this fucking beast."

The three of them held her up, giving her their strength and power, helping her. Their energy all unique, different. Heat and coolness, peace and joy breathed with her. She wasn't alone. She could do this. Had to do this. None of them would survive long if this monster wasn't destroyed. Kevin could be permanently scarred.

She glanced at the demon lying beside her. Remembered his love, his touch, how he changed Tarrin's diapers without complaint. His soft voice and his laugh.

Inhaling a deep breath, she pushed her power forward,

gathering Ben, Ralph, and Simon's along with it. All three men dropped to their knees with her from the strain.

"Go back to hell!" She shoved the magic out to the creature.

The last of the circle's candles extinguished along with the monster exploded into a million fragments, coating them and the entire room.

Her ears still rang. Throbbing pain pierced her skull. Would any of them be able to hear again normally? Or would the pain never fully go away?

"Kevin," she whispered, crawling over to him.

"He'll be okay." Ralph squeezed her shoulder. "Let's get this gunk off of us now."

"What about the ritual?" Ben asked.

Splatters of ooze from the creature covered everywhere. Even dripping from the ceiling. Kevin sat up, shaking his head. His skin was still pale but the bleeding from his ears, eyes, and nose had stopped.

"We need to find out who took Tarrin. Did you say this would narrow down which demons were responsible?" Ben took Asi's hand helping her stand.

Simon shook his head, his gaze moving from his brother to Asi. Her heart fell to her feet. He knew as she did the two beings who had done this. And that made her sick to her stomach. Made her want to ask the earth to swallow her up. She would never put Tarrin in harm's way and she'd never side with Lucas. There had to be some mistake.

"I don't know what we can do now." Ralph rubbed the back of his neck. "We can take a visit into hell and stir up some demons. I know a few who were sympathetic to our cause but wouldn't side with us while Lucas was alive. Now that he's gone that might be willing to talk."

"What about Jenna?" Ben added. "If she's recovered

enough she could identify who came or how many. Something."

"No, we don't have to do any of that." Asi wrapped her arms around herself. Her soul felt like it was being ripped in two. Once she told them, they would hate her. How could they look at her the same after she told them about the visions of the future? Surely, they would hate her.

"What do you mean?" Ralph asked helping Kevin stand.

Simon swallowed and hung his head. "I-I checked all the futures. Every one of the visions that showed what would happen to Tarrin—"

"Let me tell them," Asi interrupted.

Simon took her hand and offered her a small smile. How he could bear to touch her, she didn't know. If the vision had shown Simon or one of the others had done this to Tarrin… she didn't know if she would ever forgive them much less try to comfort them.

Kevin, Ben, and Ralph stared at her intently. And she was going to break their hearts. That realization sent bile burning up the back of her throat. They deserved to know the truth, even as ludicrous as it was.

"The reason we don't have to do another ritual or talk to any demons to find out who did this is Simon's visions." She looked from Simon's forlorn expression to his brother, Ben's, who was creased with worry. What would he think when he found out the truth? Kevin looked angry enough to crush skulls and Asi backed up a step. He'd never hurt her but what would he do when he found out the truth? Even easy-going Ralph held an expression of concern and dismay.

She swallowed against the growing boulder in her throat. "Is because it was Lucas?"

"That's not possible," Kevin growled.

"I know." God, she wanted to die. Let an earthquake happen right here and now and swallow her up. Bury her, take away her pain, her shame. She exhaled a deep breath, gathering her courage. “But in the visions, I was standing beside Lucas.”

She couldn’t say the rest. About how Tarrin lay lifeless at their feet while she and Lucas celebrated his return.

ASI

One by one, Ralph, Ben, and Kevin's emotions flashed across their features. Disbelief. Sorrow. Grief. Anger. Each one cut into a chunk of her soul.

"No," Kevin's whisper tore at her heart. "Y-you wouldn't… couldn't…"

"Your visions are wrong." Ralph growled. "Try again."

"He did." Asi stepped between Ralph and Simon. "So many possible futures that it nearly destroyed his mind. We can't dwell on how this is possible but we have to stop it. We have to get Tarrin back."

No matter what. Her son was more important than her life. If she was responsible for harming him… she shivered as her heart folded in on itself. She'd give up her life to keep him safe. Whatever it took.

Ben kept shaking his head. "I don't believe it. You wouldn't harm our baby and you certainly wouldn't bring Lucas back from the dead. There has to be something we're missing. Could demons have messed with your gift, Simon? Planted false futures?"

"That's a possibility. How do we find out if that's the case or not?" Simon pulled Asi to his side. "And if my gift of seeing the future hasn't been tampered with then we need to figure out why my visions were showing me the same thing. I don't understand and I sure as hell don't believe it but we need to move forward with the possibility that Lucas is or soon will be resurrected."

Asi swallowed against her raw throat. "Simon's right. Let's move forward with what we know. How can we find out if Lucas is resurrected? Or will be?"

Ralph rubbed his chin. "Yeah, I can make inquiries in hell and find out if anyone's heard anything."

"While he's doing that, I can research reveal spells and see if there's any magic that's been done on Simon in the last few months to double check if anyone tampered with his powers." Kevin paused in the doorway. "In the meantime, let's get this shit off us."

"I'll second that." Ben yawned. "Dawn is in less than an hour, and I do not want to fall into my day-sleep looking and smelling like this. We stink like rotten eggs."

Asi chuckled. Unbelievable that her men still wanted to stand by her after what they'd heard. She was the luckiest woman in the world. "All right. Let Simon and Ben get cleaned up first."

"You after them." Ralph grasped her hand and pulled it to his chest. "And sleep when they do."

When she opened her mouth to protest, he narrowed his dark eyes.

"I mean it, Asi. While Ben and Simon are in their vampire comas, you need to sleep."

"But I can help too," her voice was rough and came out a whisper. How did any of them expect her to sleep when her son was missing? That he could be crying and hurt right now? Sorrow welled up in her chest and she choked out a sob.

He cupped her cheek, and Simon squeezed her shoulder gently. "I know you can, love. But we need you strong and you've not slept in almost twenty-four hours. Kevin will be here doing research so he can look after you."

His compassion for her—from all of them—made her feel like she wasn't alone in this nightmare. They would stand beside her comewhatmay.

After all four of them showered, Ralph tucked Asi into their bedroom. Ben and Simon on either side of her. The sleepy tea Ralph had made for her warmed her up but now she was having a hard time keeping her eyes open.

Windows in their bedroom were shut tight with dark curtains and an added protection for her vampires against the sun of tinted windows and shutters. Shadows flickered across her bedroom from the lamp as Ralph bent over and kissed her lips softly.

He smelled of soap and smoke. Must have snuck out and had one of his cigars while she was scrapping the goo off of herself.

"Hurry back and be safe, please." She wrapped her arms around his neck to keep him leaning over her.

"I will, love." He kissed her again. "Always. Get some rest and I should have some answers in a few hours."

Yawning, she nodded.

Beside her, Ben and Simon's eyes closed and their breathing slowed. It always mesmerized her how they went from fully alive to statues and vise versa.

"Goodnight, Asi," Ralph eased her hands from his neck and placed them under her blanket.

He clicked the light off but before he could close their bedroom door behind him, Asi was asleep.

Nightmares plagued her filled with Lucas' laughter. He had Tarrin, she didn't know how, but she knew he did. Then her dream shifted to Jenna trapped in a black iron cage. She screamed, rattling the cage, but the bars burned her skin. Tears streaked down her face.

But try as she might, Asi couldn't make out what she was saying. A figure in a black cowl drifted into view and Jenna whimpered, shrinking back to the far end of the cage. She shook her head, her eyes wide with fear.

Panic slammed into Asi as though she were feeling everything Jenna was. Half her face and arm on fire. An intense pain shooting through her chest as though she was having a heart attack.

ASI

"We need to check on Jenna." Asi rubbed her arms from the chill in the air. The nightmare of feeling her friend's pain a dull ached in her chest. She could only hope that her friend had recovered enough to tell them what happened and that hopefully, Asi's weird pain was only a dream from lack of sleep and stress.

Including some clue that would help Asi and her men figure out how Lucas was resurrected with Asi beside him in the future. Her gut clenched. *There is no way that can be me.* It had to be a mistake—trickery somehow done on Simon's gift because Asi would rather die than see the lord of demons alive again. And Tarrin. She covered her mouth with a trembling hand. Why would she ever allow harm to come to her son? What could happen that would make her do that?

Guilt burned in her throat at not telling her men about the dream that felt so real or that she'd felt Jenna's pain. They'd worry and refuse to let her go to the hospital and she couldn't sit here doing nothing.

"That's a good idea." Ralph brushed a hand across her

shoulder. "Why don't you, Kevin and Ben go see her. Simon and I will stay and clean up the nursery in the meantime."

"Thank you." Asi stepped up in her tiptoes to kiss him lightly on the mouth, her insides twisting at not telling them the entire truth. Then she gave Simon a hug and quick kiss. "Be careful handling the demon ooze or whatever that stuff is."

Best she check on Jenna to figure out what the hell had happened.

The hospital buzzed with people as Asi, Ben, and Kevin strode toward Jenna's room. Many of the nurses gave Asi's escorts a double-take. Both were handsome. Ben with his brown hair that liked to sweep to the side and hazel eyes. While Kevin with his model looks were just as intriguing.

"May I help you?" a nurse at the front desk on intensive care asked.

"Yes, we are here to see Jenna Kingsley." Asi's chest constricted with worry. On the way to the hospital, Ben had called to find out if Jenna was awake or not. The nurse said she woke late last night.

"Ah yes, she is in room 1205 but visitation is limited."

Asi nodded and gave the nurse a smile though anxiousness spiked in her chest. "We won't be long," Kevin said, keeping his voice low and Asi suspected it was for the benefit of the patients nearby.

"Are you family members of Jenna?"

"No," Ben leaned on the counter, "but she's Asi's best friend and watches our son."

The nurse frowned. "I'm afraid that's not possible for you to see her if you're not relatives. Once her condition improves more, then you'll be able to visit."

"Please," Asi squeezed her hands together. They had to see Jenna. Ensure she was all right despite the demon attack and find out more information about what happened. "Please, we just need to pop in and see her. Make sure she's okay. Her and I have been friends since we were kids."

Not entirely true. She and Jenna were friends when they were in elementary school together, but then Jenna moved away with her folks and only returned three years ago. They had stayed in touch though.

The nurse paused a moment. "Five minutes is all I can give you."

"Thank you so much." Asi rushed down the hallway with Kevin and Ben behind her.

She skidded to a stop outside Jenna's room. Her heart beating so fast she didn't know if it would ever return to normal again. Slowly, she pushed the door open so as not to startle her friend.

Jenna lay in bed with half her face bandaged and gauze wrapped around her head and arm. Wires connected her to a machine monitoring her vitals. An IV bag dripped continuously along with another line for medications.

Her insides twisted at seeing her friend in such a horrible state, all because they'd asked her to babysit. If they hadn't… if Asi herself hadn't wanted to have a night out…then nothing of this would've happened. Asi and her men would've been home to defend Tarrin with their last drop of blood.

"Jenna?" Now that Asi was here, shame clawed up her throat at how hard she must have fought that demon.

The pulse meter leapt several bleeps as Jenna opened her one good eye, the other closed, swollen with purple and green bruising around it. "Asi? I'm so sorry," her voice was ragged, "I tried to stop them."

"I know you did." Asi sat on the edge of the hospital bed

and clasped Jenna's bandaged hand lightly. "Thank you. And we'll do whatever it takes to get you better."

A knot formed in Asi's stomach. Before Tarrin, she'd been consumed with learning magic to attack and defeat Lucas. Then after their son was born, she hadn't practiced any magic at all. She had no clue of how to help her friend much less heal her.

Jenna swallowed hard, an expression of pain crinkling her brow. “D-did you find Tarrin?”

“No,” Kevin answered. “But I’m sure we will soon.”

Ben stood with his hands behind his back at the far side of the room. Probably because he needed to feed soon and could smell the underlining scent of blood all around him. “Do you remember anything from the night you were attacked?”

“The doorbell rang, and I opened the door. A kid was standing there, selling something in tiny boxes. Then the child morphed into a…thing…a demon and attacked me.” Her voice cracked. “I tried to fight it off but whenever it touched me, my flesh sizzled. God, it hurt so bad. I passed out until I woke up in here early this morning.”

Asi flinched. The same time as she’d felt the intense pain like someone had taken a sledgehammer to her chest. Ben raised an eyebrow at her in question but she concentrated on Jenna.

“Did the demon have any distinguishing marks?” Kevin asked.

“Like a birthmark or something?” Jenna’s face scrunched up in concentration.

“Sometimes demons had tattoos or emblems detailing their clan.”

Jenna frowned and shook her head. “No. I don’t—wait—it had a symbol. God, why can’t I remember what it looked like?”

The heart rate monitor beeped, showing Jenna's pulse rising. One of the nurses burst into the room.

"You're upsetting the patient," she said. "I'm afraid you'll have to leave now."

"Please just one more minute," Asi said to the nurse, then leaned forward and gave Jenna a hug. "Anything at all will help us. I believe in you. Help us find Tarrin before it's too late."

Instead of answering, Jenna began to convulse. The nurse pushed Asi out of the way and pressed the alarm button. Jenna's heart rate shot from erratic to flatline. In seconds, more nurses and two doctors rushed into the small room. They placed paddles on Jenna's chest to send the electric current into her to bring her back to life.

"Jenna!" Asi cried. *No, no, no!* This couldn't be happening. Her friend had to live. Had to survive this or Asi would never be able to forgive herself for putting her in this position. An ache burned in the pit of her stomach.

As a nurse ushered them out of the room, Asi pressed her hand to her breastbone. Was her dream prophetic then? And they weren't any closer to finding out which demonic group took Tarrin than when they started.

BEN

Asi paced back and forth in the ICU waiting room, stress and fear radiated off her in waves that threatened to blow the hospital apart if someone didn't come and tell them about Jenna soon.

And who would blame her? Ben pressed his fingers to his temples. Even he was having a hard time dealing with everything. His own son, Tarrin, gone. He still couldn't wrap his brain around that someone…something had taken him or why. And if his son was hurt…he clamped down on his mounting anger before he tore apart everyone in this place.

Being here, in the hospital, was a mistake. Worse. The scent of blood was everywhere, and he trembled with the hunger burning through him. How much longer could he resist before he barged into a room and gorged on blood?

When had he last drank any? The evening before his son had been taken, he'd forgone blood to take Asi out for dinner and ended up returned to a fucking nightmare. Tarrin didn't deserve this. Hell, he was an innocent babe. Pain hit Ben's middle and he wanted to vomit. His son. Their son. Gone.

Asi and they had defeated Lucas. They'd earned a life with

happiness and in one evening it was stolen from them. Whoever had done this was going to pay. Ben would personally rip their head off and crush their bleeding heart in his hand.

Blood.

Even nauseated with the sorrow of his son on his mind, the call of it still drew him. He could resist for a bit but that might put Asi at risk. No, he'd need to sneak away soon and feed. He ran a hand across his short, cropped blond hair fighting the urge to visit the blood supply here at the hospital.

"Asi, you're swaying on your feet," Kevin said, standing. "Have a seat and let me bring you some coffee."

I glanced up to find Asi pale. She looked like she was about to pass out and here he'd been concerned with his vampire thirst to notice her pain. Guilt flooded him. He should be consoling her, hunting for their son, not wrapped up in his own comfort.

"Right. We'll grab you a bagel or something too. When was the last time you ate something?" Ben rose in hopes of regaining his chivalry and taking care of his wife too.

"No, no, I'm fine." But she did sit in one of the empty seats.

"Stay here with her." Kevin moved to the door out of the waiting room. "I'll be back in a bit with coffee and something to eat."

Mind picking up a blood bag? He wanted to add but didn't. His focus should be on Asi and her worry over Jenna, not his own comforts.

"W-What do you think...I mean... will Jenna be okay? What if she never recovers?" Guilt laced Asi's voice as she drew her legs up and sunk further in on herself in the visitor chair.

"Everything will work out." He lied because he couldn't

tell her the truth that he didn't know. That even if he wanted to and gave Jenna his blood, there was no guarantee that vampirism would take. Few of the human population survived, which was why Ben still held a hatred for his brother's ex-girlfriend who had bitten Simon. He, himself, had demanded she bite him too. No way was he going to allow his younger brother to experience such pain of transformation without him. Whatever the hell his brother was going to go through, he wanted to help him. She refused.

In the end, Simon couldn't resist the hunger and accidentally turned Ben, himself. "I'm sure Jenna is getting the best care possible."

He wrapped his arms around her, holding onto her while she cried. Half an hour later, she pushed back and rubbed her nose.

"Thanks."

"Any time." He gave her a small smile. Where was Kevin with that coffee and food? "Hey, mind staying here a sec while I go check on your other husband?"

She grabbed a tissue from the visitor's waiting room and nodded. "That would be great. As much as I don't feel like eating, my stomach feels like it's starting to gnaw on my other organs."

"Be right back." He pushed open the door, the hospital smells of bleach, cleaner, sickness, and the sweet, coppery scent of blood struck him. Now was not the time for his hunger. If Kevin had returned by now, then he could run out to the woods nearby and hunt a rabbit or deer to tide him over. Hospitals allowed vampires to come and get donated blood but there was loads of paperwork to fill out including a registered vampire license which he'd been meaning to renew but hadn't had a chance with Lucas and everything since then.

For a few brief months, his life had been perfect. Sharing

Asi with the other three guys went smoother than he'd have thought. They were a clan. A family. And each fit with Asi in their own way. He felt loved. Special. When he was with her, only he and she existed even though he knew she had three other husbands.

Her pregnancy was uncomplicated and Tarrin was a joy even if he did stress them out all the time with his weird breathing at night. Periodic breathing the doctor had called it when Ben phoned him in the middle of the night. Tarrin would breathe in, breathe out, then stop. Nothing. Nada. Then gasp in a breath and repeat. Ben had been so worried that he'd laid on the couch, holding Tarrin on his chest while the babe slept so that Asi, Kevin, and Ralph could sleep during the night shift. His brother, Simon would play video games while Tarrin lay on his chest.

The loss of his son sent a sharp pain spiraling into his gut. Tarrin. He would sell his soul to bring his child back. Whoever took him would have the greatest torture he could imagine and die the most painful and slow death possible. Just to ensure they'd have a chance at more, Ben would turn them into a vampire. If they survived the transformation, then he'd start up the torture again until nothing was left of them but a burned-out husk. Anger burned hot and bright in his chest. His skin felt tight and the urge to kill something rushed through his veins.

He turned to corner toward the hospital's cafeteria when the scent of Kevin's blood smacked into him. *What the hell?*

The smell was coming from an empty-looking hospital room at the end of the hallway with the door partially open. No lights were on.

Carefully, he rushed to the room. If someone was attacking Kevin than he wanted to surprise the bastard. When he reached the threshold, his breath froze in his chest. There was Kevin standing next to another guy. Blood ran from Kevin's wrist as the newcomer slurped up the life-giving substance. But it wasn't a vampire getting off on taking Kevin's blood. No, it was a goddamn fucking demon. A red-skinned creature with black wings and two small horns jutting out of its head. Chiseled muscles spread across its chest that even a muscle-head would envy.

"What the fucking hell?" Ben kicked the door closed behind him.

Kevin jumped, a look of shame flashed across his face before he schooled his features. The demon, obviously male by the erection jutting out from the black hair curling around his junk, disappeared from the room leaving the bitter scent of sulfur.

"I-I…uh," Kevin muttered.

"What the holy hell are you doing? And with the enemy?" Ben shoved a hand into Kevin's chest. Sickened with the fact that Kevin's obvious enjoyment of the exchange was evident in the tenting of his jeans. "We're supposed to be helping Asi. Finding our son. Tarrin. You remember him, don't you? Or are you too concerned with getting off to care?"

Kevin's face flashed red. "None of your fucking business. What I do with my own time is mine alone. I don't question you or how you get your blood—so stay out of my life."

"We made a commitment to each other and Asi, remember?" Ben growled. Was his brother initially right about Kevin? That he'd been playing them from the start? It had been him that had gotten Simon captured in the underworld even though Kevin had insisted he wasn't to blame. But someone had told Lucas they were there and that they were going after the spell book. Why else would it have been moved? And how was it they had gotten ambushed within minutes of arriving at Lucas' library?

"I know very well my vows and I was trying to help Asi."

"How?" Ben's voice rising. "By getting your jollies off with a fucking demon?"

Kevin tensed. "I *am* a demon, remember?"

"Right. And you're also married—or did you conveniently forget about that while you and it were getting hard with each other? What else have you been doing behind ours and Asi's backs?"

"Fuck you!" Kevin pushed past him to the door. "I don't answer to you."

"Well then tell Asi why you're late bringing her coffee and food." Ben snatched Kevin's elbow but the demon jerked away. "And your bite mark is healed. How long have you been doing this?"

Was he an addict? Selling information to Lucas or other demons to get his fix? *Son of a fucking bitch!*

Kevin swung open the door and strode out into the hallway. "Tell Asi I'm sorry."

And in a flash, he disappeared too, leaving Ben to pick up the pieces of what would break Asi's heart even more. Fuck!

BEN

Fucking dickhead! Ben ground his teeth. Why was he screwing around with that fucking demon? How long had they been seeing each other? Did this mean Simon was right in his original assessment that Kevin was the traitor among them? Bitterness filled the back of his throat at the thought he didn't know Kevin as well as he thought he did. The idea that Kevin betrayed them stung deeper than Ben would like to admit.

He marched to the cafeteria and picked up Asi a coffee to go and a blueberry bagel with extra cream cheese. Ben mumbled out a thank you to the cashier, his mind swirling with questions. Originally, Simon's gift of the future had shown some of the tangled lines that Kevin had betrayed them. But Kevin had proven his loyalty to Asi and the others when they battled Lucas or was it all a farce to throw them off? Learn their strengths and weaknesses. Wait until the time was right then strike when victory was assured. Why delay until now? Kevin could've shown his true colors during the battle to defeat Lucas but he fought with them.

Unless Lucas and he planned this. Some death spells

increased the power. Did Kevin plan to resurrect Lucas using Tarrin? Bring back their enemy at the cost of their son's life?

Bile burned a hole in his throat. If Kevin was involved in the kidnapping or harming one hair on Tarrin's head, Ben would rip him apart. He didn't care that Asi loved him—the bastard would be dead.

But if Kevin was innocent, then why keep this a secret? He wasn't gathering information from the demon or hell even roughing it up to figure out where their son was. Nope. He was aroused and then embarrassed when Ben had burst in on their…whatever it was they'd been doing…or about to do. Ben shivered. Gross.

He made his way back to the ICU waiting room and handed Asi her food and drink.

"Thanks. Where's Kevin?" she asked.

It wasn't his place to tell her. Let Kevin confess all his dirty secrets but he couldn't leave her in the dark forever. Still the idea of telling her, hurting her with Kevin's secret made him feel like his insides were burning up. He couldn't do it. Couldn't be the one to hurt her. She'd already gone through so much.

"Um, he needed to take care of something. He should tell you all about it when he gets back." And he needed to share what he'd found with the other guys soon if Kevin didn't come clean so they could plot what to do next. For Asi's sake, he hoped there was a logical explanation and Kevin hadn't turned on them. Ben sat beside her, curling his fists in his lap so he could keep his voice steady. "Any news about Jenna?"

"Yes," she breathed out, her breath blowing across the coffee. "She's stable but they put her into a medical coma for now until they figure out what happened."

"That's partially good news then." He forced a smile. "Let her body heal more."

Asi blinked back tears. "I know. I know I should be

relieved that she's okay. But part of me wants to scream. We're no closer to finding out who took Tarrin than we were before. She was a lead that now we can't talk to." Her hand shook and he took the coffee from her before she spilled it on herself. "I-I don't know how much longer I can hang on. I feel like my entire being is flying apart in a million directions a-and I'm barely keeping the pieces together."

"It's okay, it'll be okay." He wrapped his arms around her, drawing her in close. Good thing Kevin wasn't there right now or he'd punch him black and blue. How dare the bastard keep secrets from them…from Asi. And even if for one faction of a second, he was responsible for Tarrin's disappearance, Ben would slay him until there wouldn't be anything left of him for hell.

After Asi's crying subsided, Ben pulled back a bit. "Hey, you need to eat something, okay? We'll find Tarrin and bring him back but to do so, I do know that you need to be at your full strength. Magically and physically." Her emotional and mental states would improve once they had their son back. But in the meantime, she needed nourishment and rest.

"You're right. Thanks." She tore off a piece of bagel. "What about you? Aren't you do for a feeding soon?"

The image of Kevin giving blood to another demon crashed through him. Not that Ben gave a rat's ass about demon blood. It was highly addictive to vamps and turned them into mindless slaves to their demon masters. No, what made him fume was the fact the obvious sexual stigma between the two demons and that Kevin hadn't told Asi or the others about this. They'd sworn vows during the wedding to be faithful and exclusive to Asi alone. Kevin sneaking around doing this meant that he was betraying Asi and them. Was he going to leave? Had he really orchestrated the kidnapping? Ben pushed down his anger before Asi noticed something was amiss with his mood besides hunger.

"Oh no, I'm good for a few more hours before things get dicey."

Asi lifted her silvery-white hair off her shoulder. "I can give you blood if you need. So you don't need to wait or babysit me if that's why you've not fed yet."

Her offer made his throat clamp. Very few individuals were comfortable with a vampire feeding from them. That's why many donated blood so the vampire saliva wouldn't touch them. It was too easy for a vamp to lose control and drain the person completely. Or in some cases, too much venom in the host's system through the bite and the change into a vampire would start. Which is why vamps had to be registered in order to get blood from humans or any other being.

"Thank you." He pulled her hand to his mouth, kissing her palm. "You don't know how much that means to me."

Through her red-stained eyes, her soft half-smile sent his heart racing. She was so beautiful on the inside and out. And he was the luckiest vampire in the world that she loved him back.

A doctor entered the waiting room. "Are you Jenna's family?"

"Yes," Ben answered before Asi could say anything. He was done with this shit of not knowing anything. Playing by the rules sucked and right now, they needed answers, not red tape just because they weren't related.

"I just wanted to let you know that she's stabilized. Should be ready to wake her from the medical coma early next week."

"Thank god." Asi breathed out.

"Best thing you folks can do now is say prayers and make sure the nurse has your contact information." The doctor tucked his hands in his pockets. "You're welcome to check on her and visit her as much as you like. Sometimes coma patients remember things that were said—so try to speak positive whenever you are in the room."

"We will," Asi said, "thank you for letting us know she's holding on."

After the doctor left, Ben turned to Asi. "Finish your breakfast. We'll stop by Jenna's room for a bit then call Ralph. Maybe he and Simon have had better luck than us."

"And get you some blood, somehow."

He shrugged though the hunger was burning a hole in his stomach. For now though, he could wait a bit longer. Asi needed to see her friend. Reassure herself that her questions hadn't harmed Jenna.

RALPH

Blood coated his hands. Demon blood. Black. thick, and sticky. Ralph pushed down his revulsion to punch the demon again. This was the fifth one they'd captured and none of the others had told them a fucking thing about who had taken Tarrin. Ralph's nerves felt raw as though they'd been flayed open. Time felt like it was speeding too fast and pulsed against the inside of his skull.

Before him, the demon's hands were chained behind its back as it glared at Simon like the vampire would make a tasty appetizer.

"Tell us who worked to kidnap our son and the pain will end," Ralph growled out. He was a doctor for shit's sake. Studied for decades to learn to help and heal people. Even though his human family tried various exorcisms when they discovered he was part demon. Well, part changeling too, which to many was the same as a demon. His reward for being the perfect son for thirteen years. Hit puberty and his crimson-colored eyes showed up along with growth and muscles nearly overnight. That's when he found out holy water was a bitch. It was like being cooked in acid. Never thought he'd torture another demon with it but this one wasn't talking and Ralph would do anything to get his son back.

The demon shook its head, eyes narrowing. "Even if I did know, I'd never tell you, traitor. You've turned your back on your own kind for a filthy human."

Ralph smacked the demon in the face again and again. His rage boiling over. How dare this monster insult his wife. If he wasn't sure this creature had information, he'd rip out its heart and shove it down the demon's throat.

"Tell us who did this!" Simon dragged a chain behind him across the dusty warehouse floor.

Without asking, Ralph knew that it had been doused in holy water and consecrated. He flinched as Simon approached unable to stop himself. Too many painful memories of priests and failed exorcisms coursed through him. His arms and back still held the scars. It was only thanks to his dark skin that helped camouflage them.

Not waiting for the demon to respond, Simon whipped the chain across its legs, the links wrapping around its cloven feet. Its screech vibrated through the warehouse.

"One more time, tell us something useful or I flay your skin off." Simon jerked on the chain.

The demon's flesh sizzled and smoked, bringing the stinky order of sulfur and blood filling the air. It screamed again, its breaths turning into pants, then laughs. "You all will die when the lord rises again."

"Wait!" Ralph grabbed Simon's hand to prevent him from swinging the chain at the demon again. "What lord? Lucas? How? Tell us what you know."

In answer, the demon let out a hoarse laugh. "The witch and her babe's innocent blood will be spilled at the dark moon and the lord will rise with his love by his side."

Tarrin! The revelation that Simon's future visions might

be true shattered his soul. Not Asi. Not their son. She would never do something like that—harm their son to bring back their greatest enemy—Lucas. Why?

Then again, his own human parents had loved and adored him. But he'd watched those emotions twist into loathing once they found out about his true heritage. How many times he'd begged them to stop the torture? That he was still their son and loved them? Not once had they listened or showed mercy. Their hearts turned to granite. Was that what was going to happen to his Asi?

Ralph shook his head. No. He wouldn't allow it. He'd do whatever it took not only to bring Tarrin back but to heal Asi so that she would never be tempted, never even consider aligning herself with Lucas to bring him back from the dead.

"Where is Tarrin now? Who has our son?" Ralph said between his clenched teeth.

"He is sheltered in the abyss for now."

"The abyss? What the hell is he talking about?" Simon frowned but ice ran through Ralph's bones.

Tarrin was locked in a place between worlds. A black hole in the underworld where few could travel and return. In fact, while Ralph had worked with Lucas, none of the demons ventured too close to the areas. Even the demon lord joked that no one returned after they slipped past the barrier. That Lucas had tossed in deserters right and left, challenging them to return as he had when the great Lucifer had thrown him in there once. How it was a place of madness. And Tarrin—his newborn son—was trapped there?

The demon chuckled. "Tell him, Ralphie. Tell him how no one or nothing comes back from the utter darkness without Lucas. So you've got a choice, help bring back the demon lord or say goodbye to your son forever."

With a roar that bubbled up from his chest, Ralph rushed

the demon. His hands wrapping around the creature's throat, crushing his windpipe, choking off its air.

"Ralph, stop!" Simon jerked on his arm but even the vamp couldn't break his hold.

The crimson light in the demon's eyes flickered to nothing and still Ralph squeezed.

"He's gone." Simon's voice sounded far away.

Even though the demon was dead, Ralph didn't feel any better. "We need to get the others. Figure out a way into the abyss and bring Tarrin back without resurrecting Lucas."

ASI

Asi chewed on her nails…something she hadn't done since she was a child after her parents had died in a car crash. No, not a wreck, Lucas had attacked them on the road. Her mom had done a spell to protect Asi and her sister to keep him from getting them. While her magic worked on us, it hadn't saved her. And every single day I cursed him for what he'd taken from me.

During her session with Ben, Asi had witnessed the entire scene through his gift. Lucas had been obsessed with her mother. Claiming that he loved her. She snorted. Sure, cared for her enough to try to kill her. No way would Asi ever consider bringing that murderer back from the dead.

She and Ben returned to an empty home. Silence rang through the rooms without her son's cries or laughter filling the place. Even all three of her men were gone as well. Something was bothering Ben that didn't seem like his normal hunger state.

"Why don't you go feed?" she asked him, hanging up her coat.

"And leave you here unprotected and alone? No chance."

"Don't worry about me. I'm so angry if anything comes into our home that isn't one of my husbands, believe me, whatever it is will beg to leave." She lifted her chin when he glowered at her words. "But I'll set up a protective shield that only you and the others can pass through."

He opened his mouth to say something, then closed it. "All right, I'll go, but I won't venture far."

Why was he being so overprotective? Sure, their son had been taken but there'd been lots of times she and Tarrin had been the only ones home. If she was a target wouldn't the demons have already tried to take her too?

Once Ben drank his required supply of blood, then the strangeness in his eyes would leave or she'd at least be able to rule out hunger.

"Deal." She sat on the couch and scrolled through her phone checking for any messages from the others. Anxiety and hope mingled in her gut in hopes they'd found who took Tarrin and how to get him back.

Jenna hadn't been able to tell them anything they didn't already know. The ritual Ralph had suggested had nearly gotten them killed and nothing else except confirmation that this was demonic and had something to do with Lucas. She shivered recalling Simon's prophetic visions of her beside the monster. It couldn't be true…ever…not in this lifetime or any other.

"Lock the doors after me," Ben called from the foyer.

She groaned getting up, her back aching from little sleep last night. Most demons could bypass a locked door but since a vampire couldn't enter a home without an invitation, she humored Ben and clicked the deadbolt into place.

Her thoughts drifted back to her son. Was Tarrin safe for now? Was he crying for her right at this moment? Maybe she should try a teleportation spell and beam herself to him. Her breath caught. Or bring Tarrin to her. That had to work. Why wouldn't it?

All she needed was a bit of time to figure out the spell and perform it. And complete it before Ben or the others returned. There was a risk to spell of the atoms not going back in the proper sequence or missing others but she'd send herself to Tarrin first. Then fight whatever had him until either it or she died.

Yes, that was the better plan. Risky as shit and none of her men would let her do this which is why she had to act now.

She raced into Tarrin's room to grab something he'd recently used. The small bedroom still had the lingering scents of sulfur, burning flesh, and mildew. Covering her mouth, she snatched up his blanket from the laundry basket.

There was no time to research or practice. Any minute, Ben would return from feeding or one of the others would arrive. They'd try and stop her from doing this. And no one, not even her four husbands, not even the gods and goddesses themselves would stop her from finding her son.

Ten minutes later, Asi sat cross-legged in her bedroom with ritual supplies. The place where she and her men had made love and conceived Tarrin. His blanket lay in her lap, his newborn scent of baby and powder lingered, tears stinging her eyes. She had to do this. What other option did they have? Nothing was working and questioning demons would take too long. Anything could be happening to Tarrin right now. What if he was being injured at this second and she did nothing?

Her stomach clenched so hard, she winced. No. She would do something now or die trying. Ralph, Kevin, Ben and Simon wouldn't stop hunting for their son so even if she failed, Tarrin would have four more chances to be rescued.

She dragged the silver dagger across her palm, hissing when the blade cut into her skin. Then she traced Tarrin's name with her blood across a white candle. She lit the flame with her magic and set it in front of her on the blanket.

"Blood of my blood, babe of my loins, show me the way to your hiding spot," she chanted concentrating on the candle flame. Her magic pulsing inside her.

Smoke danced before her forming an image of Tarrin and her heart leapt. His mix of cries and hiccups filled her ears. She struggled not to burst into tears at hearing him. For this to work, she had to be strong. If she scared him, the connection between them could sever and she might never find it again.

"Yes, that's it. Show momma where you are."

But the image wavered into a swirling trail. No, no, no. Her chest tightened and she struggled to draw in a deep enough breath to say the spell again.

"Blood of my blood, my heart's song, babe of my loins, take me to you. Across time and space, from the galaxies to the depths of the underworld and beyond, let no distance keep us apart."

The candle sputtered but Asi remained in her bedroom. *Shit!* She had been so close! "Tarrin!" Her anguish shook her to the core.

Why couldn't she reach him? He was scared and she wasn't there to comfort him. What kind of mother was she? "Please, Tarrin, help me find you," her voice broke. "Momma's here just reach out to me."

But the silence choked her. He was so little. Helpless. What could he do?

Her palm itched from where she cut it while she watched the candle flame for any sign of her son. When the flame died out, so did her faith. She was supposed to be this powerful witch and she couldn't even do a simple spell to teleport herself to wherever Tarrin was.

Rage boiled in her veins. She knocked over the candle. It rolled across the wood floor under the dresser. She screamed in frustration at her inability and slapped her hands down on Tarrin's blanket. A sizzle snaked up her arms.

"Wha—"

Before she could finish her thought, the bedroom vanished. She tumbled into a dark whirlpool, unable to see anything but darkness. *Tarrin!* Was he in this void? Anguish tightened her heart until her pulse throbbed her skull. Suddenly, the air sucking out of her lungs from an unseen force. Lucas' laughter echoing around her.

BEN

Blood coated the inside of his mouth, soothing his hunger but not his anger. Ben pushed aside the now dead coyote he'd found in the woods. Humans or other supernatural beings were preferred but this was the best he could do under the circumstances. Though, he'd never drink demon blood. That stuff made too many vampires slaves and sometimes other beings too, even witches.

Asi!

Could that be what happens in the future and why Asi would side with Lucas to bring him back at the expense of their son?

Revulsion punched him in the gut. No. Asi would never… not even if compelled or bewitched. She would fight with every atom of her being to save Tarrin.

At a small creek near their home, Ben washed off the animal's blood from his hands and face. Asi knew he and his brother were vampires but he didn't want to show up looking like he'd just gorged on an animal. He jogged back to the house and pushed open the front door.

"Asi?"

An eerie silence answered him. It was almost tangible, reaching out and gripping his heart with icy fingers. She wouldn't have left, not without leaving a note or text or something. Quickly, he checked his phone. No messages from Asi just Ralph saying they had a lead and were on their way home.

Ben checked for her in the living room and the guest bathroom. Their bedroom door was closed. Dread spread through his chest even though he told himself that she was fine. Just taking a long-needed nap or an early bath.

He slowly opened the door, hopeful that the fear clawing up his throat was unjustified. Asi! The sweet scent of her blood filled his nostrils. He kicked open the door wide, rushing inside.

"Asi!" There was no sign of her. A blade lay on the wood floor. Its tip was tinged red. Ben picked it up and inhaled the aroma of his Asi. The blood was still slightly wet. She'd been cut less than a few minutes ago. Fear raked open his heart. Had someone taken her? But there were no tracks or trails of her scent that he could make out. His stomach dropped but he clenched his fists ready to fight whoever did this. Had Kevin shown up and she tried to fight when she realized he'd betrayed them?

Rage ignited in his veins and he whirled toward the door. "Asi!"

Ben tore through the house, trying to find her scent and the trail she'd have left. He wasn't a werewolf but he was a decent tracker. Even before he became a vampire, none of the kids could hide from him because he had a knack for finding them too soon. Add in his heightened vamp senses and he'd find her. Whoever took her only had a short head start and one thing was certain, he didn't smell anything foreign in their bedroom. Which meant it wasn't another demon that took her but someone familiar like Kevin wasn't out of the realm of possibilities. And that demon was going to get his skin flayed off with a chainsaw if he had done any of this.

Outside, Ben glanced back over his shoulder one more time. Hoping that he'd been wrong and Asi had been tucked away somewhere and would call out to him. He ran smack into another person.

"Hey!" Ralph grunted. "What's going on?"

Ben shook his head, afraid if he said the words they'd be set like dry cement and no chance of molding them into something else. But he had to let the others know. He looked from Ralph to his brother Simon, his heart breaking inside.

"It's Asi. She's gone. I-I think someone took her." How could he breathe with his love and their son missing? His chest hurt so hard he glanced down to check there wasn't a stake buried in his heart.

"Who?" Simon and Ralph asked in unison.

"I'm not sure." Ben clamped down on his rising panic. "There's no new scents in the house but I found a dagger with her blood on it in the bedroom."

Simon pushed past Ben into the house.

"Did you hear anything? What happened exactly?"

"No sounds," Ben shook his head. "I was out feeding and oh god, what if what took Tarrin grabbed her too?"

Ralph grabbed Ben's arm, squeezing hard. "What do you mean you don't know? Where is Kevin? I don't sense him around. Don't tell me you left Asi alone and vulnerable!"

Of course, Ralph was right but that didn't mean Ben had to like the fact himself was just as guilty.

"Look, I don't know where the fuck Kevin is. Maybe you should ask him why he bailed on us back at the hospital. And I didn't have a choice. If I didn't feed, I'd be a danger to Asi. She assured me that she'd put up a protective spell. Shit! I was gone less than half an hour."

"It only takes seconds for something bad to happen," Ralph gritted out between his teeth. "If she's hurt, I'll personally show you all thirteen levels of hell myself."

"Nine levels." Ben swallowed.

"No. Even Dante's human mind couldn't fathom all the torments of hell." Ralph dropped his arm and stalked inside the house.

Well, this day had gone from bad to horrible in a flash. All Ben wanted was Tarrin and Asi back. To enjoy their family where their greatest concern was who was going to change Tarrin's poopie diapers. He'd sell his soul and volunteer for every one of the stinky bastards if it meant having his life back the way it was before.

Too much had happened in such a short time. Now that Asi was missing and Kevin hadn't returned, they were shit out of luck.

He tucked his hands into his pockets, guilt gnawing on his insides as he followed after Simon and Ralph already in the house.

The two men stood in the bedroom, the bloody knife laying on the floor between them.

"Anything?" Ben asked.

"There doesn't seem to be any sign of struggle." Simon backed up a few steps, checking the empty area between the bed and the dresser. "No stench of sulfur like a demon took her. Sorry, no offense Ralph."

He nodded. "I don't detect anything amiss either."

"What the fuck happened?" Simon clenched his fists. "Check with Kevin—maybe he knows something—or at least tell him what's going on."

"Too bad Ralph can't read his mind," Ben mumbled. Then they'd know where the bastard stood. But Ralph's power, when he chose to use it, only allowed him to freeze time and read vampire's minds—not demon's or any other creature's.

"What do you mean?" Ralph picked up the blade, narrowing his gaze at the bloody tip.

Shit! He heard me. "Just what I said."

Ralph laid the blade on top of the dresser. In a flash, he held Ben up by his throat. "We don't have time for games, little vamp, tell me exactly what you are talking about."

"Wha—!" Simon yelled but his body froze mid-run with Ralph's power of stopping time hitting him.

"Unless you want me to stop your heart, talk," Ralph's voice lowered an octave.

"How do you expect him to answer you if you're pressing on his windpipe?" Kevin asked leaning against the door-frame. Next to him stood the demon from the hospital with black wings and in its hand was one of Tarrin's pajamas.

The room tilted beneath Ben as Ralph dropped him and dove for Kevin and the newcomer.

KEVIN

Kevin let Ralph take a swing at him. The punch landed on his chin and nearly knocked him off his feet. What the holy hell? If he'd know he'd get this kind of greeting, he'd have stayed with the incubus back in the underworld for the night.

"First one's free, now it's my turn," Kevin spat out a string of blood. "Someone want to tell me what the fuck is going on?"

"You!" Ralph reared back his fist. "I saw everything from Ben's mind. You betrayed us!"

Shit! "It's not like that." Kevin held up his hands in surrender but he kept them near his head. No way was he going to get punched again without fighting back.

"Maybe this is a bad time, I can come another day." The incubus scooted back from the door.

"No, no, you're not going anywhere." Ralph tossed out his power, freezing time around the incubus before it'd vanish.

"Will someone explain what the hell is going on?" Simon shouted. "It's like I've entered the Twilight Zone meets Buffy the Vampire Slayer and I'm completely lost."

"Tell them." Ben challenged.

This would've been so simple if the vampire hadn't caught him but he'd save that secret reveal for when they were all together. "Fine. Where's Asi, she needs to hear this too."

Simon's face fell and Kevin's heart slammed against his chest.

"Asi's missing." Ralph marched to the dresser and picked up a dagger. "This was all we found. It was here in the bedroom laying on the floor. And where the hell were you?"

"What? Missing? I left her with Ben." He whirled on the vampire. "None of this would've happened if you had minded your own business."

Ben yelled throwing a punch into Kevin's face. "Bastard! You fucking traitor! I knew we couldn't trust you. My brother's predictions were true."

"No." Simon stepped between them. "I can't believe that. Not after all this time. He proved himself during the battle why would he turn now?"

The fact the vampire held hope in his eyes, hit a chord in Kevin's heart. Neither vampire brother had been thrilled at first to be working with two demons but they'd come around for Asi's sake. They were a family. Bound to Asi. Each sharing her heart and yet uniquely making it bigger rather than taking pieces.

Simon had been the one before that had been leery of him after his visions showed Kevin siding with Lucas. But deep inside, Kevin knew that would never happen. He'd trusted the bastard once until Lucas had killed his vampire fiancée. Then Kevin had made it his mission to destroy Lucas.

"So, why the other demon and secrecy?" Ben motioned to the Incubus watching them with mild curiosity.

"This is Q and he has information that could help us. I was trading my blood for it." And other favors but he wanted to speak to Asi about that directly not have her other husbands ready to toss him out.

"What kind of name is that? A letter?" Ben crossed his arms, his eyes narrow.

"You wouldn't be able to pronounce his full name." Kevin resisted rubbing his chin that still ached from Ben's punch. "And even if you managed it, his name would bind you to him and you'd have an incubus invading your sleep every night."

"Spill," Ralph stalked toward Q like a black panther hunting prey. "What do you know about Lucas or Asi or our son?"

Not missing a beat, Q bowed but didn't wipe the smirk off his lips. Cheeky bastard. "I know where your son is."

"That would've been valuable information an hour ago, but we already know where he is." Ralph grabbed Q's shirt hauling him closer. "Now I'll ask you again, give us everything."

Q paled a lighter shade of red but nodded. "Ever since you guys defeated Lucas, half of hell has been rejoicing."

"And which half are you?" Ben glowered.

"I've no need for a prejudice monster running the roost." Q pried Ralph's fingers off his shirt. "I happy with the way things are now and have no wish for them to change."

Ralph let go of Q and stepped back. "Alright. But we already know Tarrin is the black abyss in hell. How do we get him out? And what do you know about Asi's disappearance?"

"Nothing on the latter, I'm afraid." Q shrugged. "Though I'd really like to have met the human witch who put Lucas down. As for the abyss, it's easy to get to…harder to get out of."

"God, does this guy ever talk logically and make sense?" Ben cursed. "I can see why you like him, Kevin."

Heat rose up into Kevin's face. He didn't want anyone to

know his true feelings. Not until he spoke with Asi. "Let's focus on getting Tarrin and Asi back, okay?"

"Fine." Ben straightened but the muscle in his jaw twitched. "What do you purpose?"

"Q is not in charge here," Ralph said in a firm voice. "I am —*we* are. Kevin and Simon will keep looking for Asi here. I'll go with Q and Ben to the abyss to see if there's a way to bring Tarrin back."

Kevin's heart beat to triple time. He'd made Q promise to keep their secret but would the incubus obey? As if sensing his worry, Q blew him a kiss. Ralph, Q, and Ben disappeared.

"Any ideas of where Asi might have gone or who would've done this?" Simon asked.

"None." Kevin shook his head. "There's no way someone could take her down without a fight. Doesn't make sense."

"What about the dagger?" Simon picked it up by the handle. Asi's crimson blood coated the tip but had crusted some. "I'm not getting any other scents but hers."

Had she cut herself on purpose? Kevin shook his head as denial raked up his throat. She'd never commit suicide—not when there was a chance of getting Tarrin back. So why the blood and blade?

He raked his hand through his dark hair, wanting to strangle someone or hit something. Jenna had been no help, unfortunately, but it wasn't her fault. A savage demon had attacked her and she was lucky to be alive at all.

"How did you and Ralph find out about the abyss," He sat down on the bed. The hope of Q helping them now sitting like a weight in his gut if Tarrin was in the abyss. They still had no way for certain to reach him. Now with Asi missing, Kevin felt like he'd been filled with lead. Unable to breathe or hell even move without feeling the crushing weight.

"A demon told us." Simon paced back and forth. "I mean I know Ralph was a demon but he always seemed so composed to me. Normal. Like a guy that would bandage you up and give you a lollipop for your pain. But when he went after the demon that taunted him," he shook his head, "he was scary."

Kevin understood. He'd seen Ralph in action before. Normally the half-demon was calm with a bedside manner that radiated off him and you couldn't help but trust him. He was a natural leader and they'd followed his advice when they were shielding Asi from Lucas and teaching her magic.

"This is a war," Kevin said, his anxiety climbing up his chest. "Ever since Tarrin was taken, we've been acting defensively. And whoever is responsible for this has been one or two steps ahead of us the entire damn time."

He'd never felt so helpless in his entire life. Asi was his air, the force and love that made his heart beat. It was as though he were in the abyss now instead of Tarrin. Floating in darkness. Alone.

"Exactly." Simon paused in his pacing. "Fuck man, it's like we do have someone snitching on us."

"Are we back to this again?" Kevin stood. He was tired of this shit. Of the others believing he would do anything that would hurt Asi or Tarrin. "I told you, I didn't set you up in the underworld. Both of us were after the spell book to help Asi. None of us knew it had been moved or that Lucas would have an ambush waiting for us."

"That's the whole point." Simon pounded his fist against his palm. "Someone knew we were going after the spellbook. And if it wasn't you then who would have had access to what we were doing?"

"Are you suggesting one of us would harm our son? Or Asi?" Fury bubbled up inside him. "None of us would do that —each of us would give our lives for them."

"Unless there was more than what we are seeing?" Simon paled like he was going to be sick. "Unless my visions were showing me that one of us has two sides—like Ralph turning into a torture master."

Kevin curled his hands into fists. "Are you accusing me of doing this? Of playing both sides until what? Tarrin was born? That's just fucking sick. Few of the worst demons in hell wouldn't even be able to stomach that."

Sacrificing his own son for what? The resurrection of the being he hated most in the universe? No thanks.

"No," Simon's whispered voice sent shivers down his spine. "Asi."

RALPH

The thought of his son in the abyss made Ralph want to leap into the darkness and rescue Tarrin. What kind of monster would throw him into a place like that? *Lucas.*

But the demon lord was dead and someone was trying to resurrect him using their son. Bring whoever it was before him now and he'd rip their bones out of the body.

Before him and Ben, the abyss pulsed like a living entity. No demons guarded the void because anyone stupid enough to venture too close would get sucked in. Anyone that fell in wasn't coming back again.

Except Lucas. He'd managed to return so there was hope for Tarrin. *Please let him be safe.*

There had to be some way of getting to their son and bringing him back.

Ben frowned at the dark, swirling hole. "Tell me you've got a plan."

"Tarrin," Ralph knelt down before the edge of the abyss, "can you hear me? We need to get to you but don't know how." It was beyond hope to think that Tarrin would respond even if he could. He was only a few months old but Ralph would've been overjoyed for a cry. Something to let them know he was alive. Anything.

"Well, well, well," a familiar feminine voice echoed from behind them. "Wondered how long it would take you to figure out the connection with your missing son and the abyss."

Ralph spun. But the image of the woman coming at him didn't register right away. It was like he saw her but his brain was trying to process exactly what he was seeing.

"Asi?" he asked, staring at her.

"No!" Ben charged but Asi snapped her fingers and the vampire flew across the chamber, crashing into a stone pillar.

Then she flicked her fingers and the vampire rose into the air. He hovered over the middle of the abyss. His eyes bulging as he struggled to move. Mumbles came out but no words. She had bound and gagged him somehow with magic.

"Asi, we found Tarrin, he—"

She rolled her eyes. "He wouldn't shut up. Like I never knew such a tiny babe could make such a fuss."

"What's going on?" Ralph looked from Ben's frantic movements that gained him nothing to her. "This isn't like you. Our son is trapped down there. We need to get him out."

"And why would I want to do that? The brat being in the abyss has strengthened Lucas—my true love—unlike you four pathetic has-beens." She sashayed to the other side of the cavern where she could watch both him and Ben at the same time.

"Asi," Ralph tried again, "Whoever took you must have you under a spell. Fight it. We love you. Tarrin loves you, he needs you...we all do."

"Oh," She pressed a hand to her heart. "I must really work harder to speed things up."

His blood ran cold. "What do you mean?" Something told him that she wasn't talking about saving their son.

"Fight this, Asi. Rememb—"

"Enough!" She clapped her hands, and an invisible hand clamped over his mouth. "Thank you for coming to me so I didn't have to lure you two out. Lucas requires more sacrifices for his resurrection."

Ralph pushed his gift of freezing time forward but nothing happened. Instead, a tightness settled around his chest and lifted him in the air until he was beside Ben over the abyss.

Why was she doing this? With his mouth sealed shut, he couldn't ask her. Could do nothing but watch his wife, the mother of his son, grin at him like she was winning at their weekly poker games. She never could keep her emotions from showing on her face despite the tips and tricks he showed her.

He forced all of his emotions, his longing, his hope that she'd snap out of this to the front. Let her see his rawness in his gaze.

But she didn't even give him a second glance. She whistled and demons came pouring out of every hide hole they'd been in. Scaling down stalactites. Some teleporting in bringing the heavy stench of sulfur and brimstone with them. Larger, wingless demons carried in a body shrouded under a black cloth.

"Soon, my love, soon we'll be reunited." She turned back to the abyss, letting out a shout in a language Ralph didn't recognize. Her hands trembled as she held them out to the abyss.

Slowly, a tendril of light oozed like a fog toward her. It undulated toward the covered body. Asi jerked her hand toward Ralph and Ben. Blood dotting their pores and slithered down to join the fog feeding whatever was under that shroud.

Ralph didn't have to guess who Asi was trying to resurrect. Lucas.

KEVIN

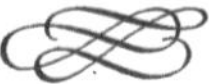

Simon kicked the edge of the bedpost. Frustration aggravating his mood. All of this shit, running around and doing ritual crap was useless. They were no closer to finding Tarrin than before. Now Asi was missing too. Aside from her being taken completely by surprise, Simon's guess was that she went willingly. But why?

Was it whoever had taken their son? Or someone she trusted who tricked her?

"This is getting us nowhere. Has Ralph or my brother sent any messages?"

Kevin shook his head but checked his phone anyway. "Nada. It's making me nervous though that we haven't heard from them."

"Yeah. Me too." They were in the underworld for fuck sake. Demon territory. While some demons like Q were cool with them, others weren't. "So what's the real deal between you and Q?"

Kevin's phone slipped out of his hand and clattered to the floor, sliding halfway under the dresser.

So there was something going on between Kevin and Q

that was more than gathering information. Was Simon wrong about the demon? Had he wanted to betray them from the start? Asi had told Simon to trust his gut not his visions so much. That the future was riddled with possibilities and choices. Kevin siding with them had proven to Simon that the demon was trustworthy but his reaction to Simon's words showed something else. It revealed a deep secret that Kevin was hiding.

The demon squatted down to retrieve his phone, then paused. "There's a candle down here."

"Asi's got a ton of them lying around." Simon shrugged. "They helped her focus her magic early on but she's way past that."

With a grunt, Kevin pushed his arm under the dresser and drew out a thick, white candle. Tarrin's name was written around it in red letters.

"Fuck!" Simon cursed. "What is that?"

"I think Asi performed a spell to find our son but it backfired."

"Meaning?" His stomach twisted into knots. What had Asi done and where was she?

"Not entirely sure but since we've no other clue what happened to her and there doesn't seem to be a struggle, I think she was teleported to Tarrin."

Simon swallowed the growing lump pressing in his throat. "So she's in the abyss? Let's go!"

Before Kevin could respond, Simon dashed out of the room. If Asi and Tarrin were in that horrible place than he was going to get them out. Even if he had to make a ladder from dead demons to do it.

Simon and Kevin paused behind the cavern's stalagmite as hundreds of demons chanted in what sounded like garbled words. Over the swirling black hole in the center of the cave, Ralph and Ben hung in midair. Blood coated their clothes. Though they trashed around, neither got free of whatever held them. Rage and fear for Asi and Tarrin rose up in his chest.

"What the fuck?" Simon took a step forward to help the others but Kevin placed his arm in front of him, blocking him off.

"Someone is drawing power from the abyss, from the guys, from Tarrin."

"Wait," Simon's throat tightened at seeing the woman in red with the silvery-white hair standing off to the side of the churning black hole. "Is that Asi?"

A shriek rose up from somewhere ahead, sending a skeletal finger down Simon's spine. Next to Asi, a body rose. *Lucas*! His golden hair matted and half his skull was showing. Where his skin was still attached was blackened and scorched. He looked like a zombie thrown in the fire a few times.

"Awaken my love," Asi purred, "Take what you need from the sacrifices."

No, no, no! This wasn't real. Couldn't be. Asi would never harm them or Tarrin. But the truth was standing a few hundred yards away. Asi went missing, she'd done a spell that brought her here and now she'd resurrected fucking Lucas.

"We have to do something. We have to stop her." Simon's chest hurt. Why would she do this? Betray them...break their vows to side with Lucas? He blinked, hoping that it was a mirage or he was seeing things wrong. But no, it was her. Same heart-shaped face, same clear, light skin. Tears clogged his throat. There had to be a reason she was doing this? Or had she been possessed? Yes, that had to be the reason. His Asi would never harm their son…never bring back Lucas. Except she didn't move as a possessed person did. They had a distinct walk like a puppet master pulled their strings and Asi moved as graceful as ever.

Would he be able to hurt the woman he loved? Yes. If it meant saving their son.

"How?" Ralph shook his head. "She's not only got all of our powers but her own as a witch."

"If we don't do something, then Tarrin and the others will die. Lucas will gain strength and power. Isn't that what all this about? Taking their sacrifice, their abilities, and giving it to him?" Shit! He'd been fucking hard to put down the first time. With Asi by his side, he'd be invincible. There had to be a way to break whatever spell was making her do this.

When Lucas' mangled hand took one of Asi's, Simon trembled with rage. He wanted to kill Lucas again for touching her. It had to be Lucas' doing somehow. Paid someone on the other side of death to attack her. Control her. Bastard had always gotten his way in the past and used whoever he could. They just had to figure out how to wake Asi up from whatever magic trapped her into bringing Lucas back.

"Where's Q?" Kevin asked, worry lacing his words, as his gaze moved from side to side.

"I thought he came with Ralph and Ben but I don't see him anywhere."

"Stay here." Kevin teleported out of sight.

Great. Just what Simon needed. Stuck down in hell with a bunch of demons and his wife turned shit-bat crazy. How much more fucked up could his life get?

SIMON

Simon wished his power was more useful like Ralph's ability to freeze time and shit. Nope. He got stuck seeing multiple futures but none showed promise as waited for Kevin to get his ass back here. None of the futures were good. They all showed Lucas at full strength and Asi by his side. Just as his gift had shown back at their home.

What good was viewing possible futures if none of them made sense? What if none brought his son back?

But he couldn't just stay hiding behind this stalagmite, watching his brother and Ralph get sucked dry. And Tarrin was somewhere in that churning abyss as well. If Simon could get Asi away from Lucas, then he could get her to snap out of whatever had messed her up. Then they'd have a chance against Lucas.

"Hey," Kevin suddenly whispered behind him.

"Fuck man, don't do that shit."

"Sorry." Kevin pointed his chin at the demon crowd. "I found Q."

"So, what's the plan?"

"He'll create a distraction, while I sneak up and grab Asi," Kevin explained.

"Wait." Simon frowned. "What do I do?"

"Help me figure out how to break whatever bewitchment is making Asi do this."

"I'm a vampire, what the hell do I know about breaking curses?" Simon wasn't ready for this. Even if he'd crammed all night he wouldn't be—he paused. Something was off about Asi. Besides her wanting to bring Lucas back and kill her husbands and child. Was it his imagination?

Simon narrowed his gaze, concentrating on Asi.

"Ready?" Kevin asked and raised his hand to signal Q.

Too late, Simon grasped Kevin's hand, bringing it down quickly. "Stop."

"We have to do this now." Kevin frowned. "Any longer and Lucas will have full power. He will win against us no matter what we do. This is our only chance."

Simon shook his head. If he was wrong about this, they we're all dead. Might as well live on the edge of danger.

"Come on, we have to move now or we lose our chance."

"What if you're wrong?"

"No, this is the only way. We have to get Asi back."

"What if we've all been wrong and Asi can't be swayed? That no matter what we do or argument or incantation we use, she won't ever stop trying to bring Lucas back." Damn. Asi is the one who told him to look beyond his prophesies and trust his gut. They'd been wrong about Kevin—so were they wrong about Asi now?

"We don't have a choice. If we don't get Asi th—"

"No." Simon glanced back at her, his voice a mere whisper. "What if that's not our Asi."

"What the hell do you mean? Of course it's Asi. Looks like her, sounds like her. Who else could it be?" His eyebrows rose in question.

"Someone I'd thought died a few years ago. Tara." Simon shook himself. If he wasn't right about this and it was indeed Asi, he would condemn them all. Fear choked him.

"Asi's twin sister?" Kevin hissed in a breath. "But she died. Absorbed too much power and died."

"That's the version we told you all. But there was more to it. She was obsessed with power. Killed two of our group before Ben and I were able to put her down."

"So how is she alive and bringing back Lucas now?"

"That's the million-dollar question," Simon said. "When we put her down before, or so we thought, she killed two others of our group plus a wizard. Ben and I barely managed to survive with powerful allies. More importantly, how do we save the others when there is no way in hell that Tara will listen to us."

KEVIN

Tara. Kevin had heard bits and pieces from Ben and Simon about her whenever Asi asked. Her grandmother had wiped Asi's memory of her sister. The spell was so strong that it remained intact even after her grandmother's death. Kevin had always thought that odd but now it made sense if Tara were alive or able to return somehow, then Asi's grandmother wanted to keep her safe. Including never attempting to contact or rise her sister from the dead.

If what Simon said was true, than they had huge problems. Tara was a witch like Asi. Powerful since she was the elder twin. Her siding with Lucas tipped the balance in his favor in a major way. And where was their Asi? Everything pointed to her being here in the underworld. Unless. Unless she was in the abyss with Tarrin, their son.

That thought should've terrified him. Instead, it gave him a sense of peace that Asi might be with their son and comforting him. But both of them along with Ralph and Ben would die if Lucas and Tara got their way.

SO, they had to stop the ritual.

"When Q makes a distraction, then we attack Tara. Knock

her down, whatever we can to sever the link between Lucas and the others."

"That's your plan?" Simon hissed. "What part of she's as powerful as Asi or more so didn't you understand?"

"You got any better ideas?"

Simon glared but after a moment, shook his head once.

"On my mark." Kevin raised his hand, signaling Q.

"Fellow demons," Q shouted. "Do you want to live in bondage and slavery again? Help me defeat our oppressor!"

Shouts of agreement rose. Demons swarmed Lucas and Tara. But many. More than Kevin would've liked stood against the onslaught, protecting Lucas.

"Now!" Kevin yelled. He and Simon shot to their feet.

They dodged demons fighting each other to get to Tara. Was that a look of amusement on her face? *Shit!*

As though shooing a fly, she flicked a hand out. Hordes of demons burst into flame. Ashes floated down like snowflakes. The power struck Kevin in the chest, knocking him backward. His insides burned and cramped like he was being burned alive. He yelled but it turned into a strangled scream as the fire seared him inside.

"Here, drink!" Simon offered his wrists. "It'll speed up your healing. "Hurry!"

Kevin clamped down on the offering, the vampire blood coating his mouth and quenching the fire inside.

"Thanks," he nodded to Simon, "Let's go stop this bitch."

The vampire's smile brightened his whole face. He helped Kevin stand. Snarls and shouts echoed around them. Together, they faced Tara, racing toward her.

Kevin knocked aside an imp that tried to bite his leg. Another demon jumped on his back, sinking its fangs into his shoulder.

"Tear them apart!" Tara chuckled.

Two grunxel demons barreled forward along with half a

dozen hellhounds. The dogs were bad enough but the hornless, ox headed grunxel were the linebackers of the underworld. They could rip Simon and him apart piece by piece. Kevin spun, kicking the nearest hound in the snout. Then he punched another in the chest as it leapt in the air at his face. Ugly bastards. Dogs with no fur and black skin pulled tight over their bones.

One of the grunxel grabbed Kevin's neck. He flung him toward a pack of fighting demons. A hellhound jumped on his back, its razor-sharp teeth chomping down on his shoulder. The grunxel lugging him up by his head. Punching Kevin in the gut over and over until he tasted blood in the back of his throat.

No! He wasn't going to stop or give up. Asi, Tarrin—their son, and the others needed him. Loved him.

Gritting his teeth against the pain shooting through him, he kicked the grunxel's chest. The momentum tore the demon's grip away. Kevin fell backward, landing hard on his hip. The air whooshed from his lungs with a grunt. But he pushed up, curling his shoulders forward, raising his fists.

"Do I have to do everything myself?" Tara sounded bored. She held out her hand, then clenched it closed.

A tightness suddenly latched onto Kevin. He couldn't move. Drawing in air was a struggle. Spots danced before his vision.

"Too bad my sister picked weaklings as her champions." She picked at her nails. "Out of all of you, only the one worth a damn has the ability to freeze time. Yet, even he couldn't beat me."

"You won't win," Simon squeezed out the words between pants. "We defeated you once and can do beat your sorry ass again."

She laughed. "That was before, when I had only absorbed

three being's power. When I'm done here, I will be unstoppable."

Her crimson gown swished as she left Lucas' side. The demon lord's flesh was healing and his skin took on a rosy glow.

Shit! Soon he'd be at full strength.

"Why are you doing this?" Kevin searched for a way to convince her this was wrong. "You prepared to fight Lucas with Simon and the others before, remember? Risked your life to get stronger because you believed in putting down a monster."

Stopping before Simon, she patted his cheek. "I never wanted to gain magic and abilities to stop Lucas but to join him. I was a spy but I got too power hunger. Yet, you couldn't stop me before—not completely. Once I have all of your powers and my nephew's, no one will be able to challenge me."

ASI

Searing pain lashed through Asi as though she was being whipped everywhere. Lashes striking all the way down to her bones. She tumbled over and over in darkness. Her head spun. Where was she?

Every time she fought to right herself and stop, she only spun faster.

Bile burned her throat. Her magic trickling out of her. Soon, she'd have nothing left.

Enough! She screamed in her mind. But the darkness only squeezed her harder. She gasped as pain shot down her spine. Thoughts scrambling.

No! She was here for Tarrin. The spell had brought her here for a reason. Her son had to be in this void. Somewhere.

Tarrin! She had to reach her son. Help him. Panic swelled in her cheat. He had to be okay. *Tarrin!*

But she couldn't hear anything beyond her pulse throbbing in her ears.

Wait. She was a witch, damn it! Something she denied for so long until her men...her four princes showed her how to accept her power and how to use it. They'd shared their magic with her. She cherished her men.

Each had a unique ability and she could use their magic now. Kevin could hear over great distances. Would she be able to figure out where her son was? Hope flickered deep in her heart.

She pushed aside the dizziness and thought of her precious son as hard as she could. *Tarrin!*

A faint cry sounded in the distance but she couldn't figure out exactly where as the darkness twisted her this way and that.

She had to reach him! Wait. Ralph's ability to freeze time. Shoving aside her nausea, she trembled trying to hold the magic and reign in time. It bucked under her control as though alive and sensing her weakness. She ground her teeth together. This had to work.

Slowly, her body spinning infinitely stopped. She gasped for breath. Part of her too frightened to blink least the magic give way and she start whipping through space again.

"Tarrin, it's momma, show me where you are." Her voice broke.

His soft cry reached her. She groped in the darkness, trying to pull herself through air until at least she touched his foot.

"Tarrin," she cooed, pulling him up to her.

But his skin was cold to the touch. Too cold. She wrapped her arms around him. Her instincts shouted for her to get out of this nightmare or she and Tarrin wouldn't survive.

Okay. So how to get out. Both Tarrin and later she had ended up here so there had to have an escape. Something. The spell had zapped her here but she had no candle to focus her power or ritual tools. All she had was herself and Tarrin. His cries softened but his body shook in her arms.

She'd been able to use both Ralph and Kevin's power to get this far. So why not teleport out of this endless darkness? It was dangerous if it did work. What if she ended up inside a brick wall or in the middle of the highway?

No, she needed to think of somewhere safe that she'd been before but she had no idea how far away it was. Best to jump somewhere closer. But she had to get them out of here now—it was worth the risk to save herself—save her son.

A man's scream echoed in her ears. Kevin! Another man yelled. Simon! Someone was hurting her men and they sounded just on the other side of this black hole.

"Hold on, Tarrin." She clutched him to her chest, closed her eyes, and thought as hard as she could what it felt like whenever Kevin or Ralph had teleported with her. How her hair stood on end and the faint smell of ozone filled her nostrils. The slight queasiness of her stomach when they moved from one place to another. But most of all, she thought of each of her men. How much she loved and missed them. How each of them adored her and Tarrin and how much she loved each of them. How special their bond was.

She gasped as her body stopped spinning and her feet landed on something solid. Her eyes flew open. The black pit was behind her and Tarrin. Over it hung Ralph and Ben both looking as pale as ghosts.

Gurgling screams came from across the cavern and she jerked toward the sound. Simon and Kevin hung in the air as huge hornless, ox-headed demons punched them. While shorter demons raked their claws down their flesh and hell-hounds snapped at their feet.

Her steps tumbled forward as she was torn who to help first.

"Look who emerged from our trap," Lucas' raspy voice snarled. "The bitch and her brat."

"Let them go, Lucas." She squared her shoulders, lifting her chin despite her fear crawling across her skin. How was it possible he was alive? The memory of Simon's visions flooding her, stealing her breath.

"Ah, that I will do, once they are dead and we've absorbed their power."

She shook her head. "Not happening. Let them go and I can promise you a quick death." Her magic churned in her gut along with her anger.

"You bested me the first time." Lucas adjusted his black robe. "But you didn't defeat me."

"Oh?" She lifted Tarrin higher on her shoulder so she could have one hand free to unleash her magic in case Lucas attacked. "Dead sounds like I did."

He laughed, but the sound grated on her nerves. "And did you think after living centuries that I wouldn't have a contingency plan? That I wasn't recruiting key players for the battle?"

"What are you talking about? Demons?" She snorted. Everywhere she saw, demons fought each other. "Looks to me like half of them are against you."

"Only because I need to finish you all off first." He shrugged. "They lack faith."

She needed to put Tarrin somewhere safe so she could fight. Free her men and then they face Lucas together like before.

"Why don't you give him to me?" Jenna asked.

"Wha—" Asi turned to find her friend standing before her in a low-cut dress that clung to her curves.

"Hurry, you don't have much time before Lucas kills your husbands."

Asi's thoughts clashed into each other. "H-How are you here?"

"Don't listen to her, it's a trap!" Kevin yelled.

But suddenly his face turned purple. He struggled for air.

"She's your—" Simon started but he too ended up struggling to speak.

"Hurry, Asi. Give me the child and all will be well."

Jenna had no marks on her face. No cuts or bruises or flayed flesh like when she was in the hospital. Was this a trap? An illusion of Lucas' creation?

"Why aren't you in the hospital?" She shook her head, backing away. Tarrin whimpering in her arms.

"I-I was healed. A witch came in and fixed me."

But there was a hard edge to Jenna's voice.

"No." Asi took another step back. There was nowhere to run to keep Tarrin safe. She was trapped and alone—her men couldn't help her—they couldn't even save themselves.

"Give me the baby, Asi." Her face turned from kindness to anger. "Don't make me ask again."

Suddenly, flashes of the past slammed into Asi. Of her life with her sister before Tara died. How her sister was always angry. Always demanding. How she bullied Asi whenever their grandmother wasn't looking.

"Tara?"

"Took you long enough, twin." Tara winked. "Maybe you're getting smarter after all these years. Too bad it's too little too late."

"Don't come near me or my son!" Asi lifted her chin despite her panic snaking through her middle. All her life, Tara had been better at everything. At hide-n-seek, at school and sports, at boys.

"Or what? You'll cry like you always did?" Tara mocked. "The baby of the family that never grew up. That mom and grams sheltered. Time you learned who I am and how I will always be your better."

Magic crashed into Asi like a wrecking ball had hit her

chest. She fell to her knees, holding onto Tarrin so he didn't hit the dirt.

Around her, demons hooted and cheered. Despair raked through her mind. She couldn't win. She'd never been able to beat Tara at anything. She'd failed. Failed her men, her son, herself.

ASI

Asi's twin sister laughed as she circled around her. Gone was the charade of her looking like Jenna. Her white hair shone against her crimson gown. She looked like a mirror image of Asi but they were nothing alike.

Her vision tunneled as pain shot through her chest but she didn't let go of Tarrin.

"My poor sister, so gullible." Tara chuckled. "So easily controlled from the sidelines."

"Wha-What are you talking about? You died." Asi shook her head, trying to clear her mind to open up her magic. But her power felt so far away. Like a chasm stood between her and the magic.

"Is that what Simon and Ben told you?" She placed a finger under Asi's chin and lifted her head up to look into her grey eyes. "No my dear, that's what Lucas and I let them think. True, they did kill my body, but my spirit came here to hell. Lucas promised me immortality with him if I did one simple thing."

"Which was?" Asi forced the words out. Her breaths labored and she was having a hard time focusing.

"Resurrect him if you bumbling fools managed to beat him." She rose, letting go of Asi's chin. "Which, I was surprised you did. Especially after I warned him that you were going after his spell book."

"H-how did you know about that?"

"You told Jenna, remember?" She clapped her hands. "Oh right. You still haven't figured that out."

"Wait, you're Jenna?" She shook her head. "No, that's not possible. I remember her. We were friends." Until Jenna moved away during eighth grade. She didn't return until... until a few months after what would've been Tara's death.

"Ah, now you get it. I took dear Jenna's place. You never questioned or once had a suspicion of me. I could always read you."

Had she told Jenna about the book? Asi frowned, trying to think, but another whip of magic struck her across the back and she doubled over.

"Like I said, you can't win against me. Never. Now hand over the baby or I will kill your men, then you, and take what I want."

Like she always had.

Asi dug for her power. Summoned her strength to attack. She couldn't let her sister do this. Even if it cost her life, Tara wasn't getting her son.

"No," she whispered.

"I'm sorry, what was that?" Tara kicked Asi in the side.

She braced herself, cradling Tarrin against her fall. Carefully she sat up.

"No," she said louder.

"Unbelievable. You are just as stupid as you were before." Tara slapped Asi so hard her teeth cracked.

Shaking, Asi pushed up to a stand. A metallic taste filling her mouth. "No."

"Stop playing with your sister and kill her." Lucas

marched toward the black hole. He held out his hands toward Ralph and Ben who's renewed muffled screams tore chunks out of her heart.

Asi let her panic and fear show on her face. She had one chance at this. If she didn't play the part perfectly, her sister would realize something was up. She squeezed her eyes shut, holding Tarrin closer, shushing him so his cries wouldn't give her away. This was the only way she could win. The only one of the possible futures she'd opened that showed a chance but it all hinged on her being able to keep a poker face. Something she'd never been able to do before. But now Tarrin's life, her men's, and her's was on the line.

Worry clamped on her heart, her breaths coming out short and hard. She had to do this. She could do this.

When another wave of magic slashed across her back, she threw herself to her side. Carefully, she laid Tarrin down. Imaging him safe in his room at home and one of his teddy bear and her silver dagger in his place.

"Please no, don't hurt my baby." She cried, feigning she was hurt far more than she was by the strike.

"Get out of my way." Tara kicked her hard.

But when her sister reached down for Tarrin, Asi forced all of her magic she could grasp forward into her sister. "I said stay away from him, bitch!"

Tara screamed as her body jerked. Heat burned bright inside her until she exploded. Pieces of her flying everywhere.

A winged demon rushed to Asi but his crimson eyes held kindness. "Let me take your son somewhere safe."

"No need." She smiled.

Lucas roar rang through the cavern. Every demon stopped.

"I will kill you all now for defying me!"

ASI

Asi stumbled but the demon who'd offered to help take her son, held her up. What was this new demon's intentions? She shook her head, she'd deal with him later if he was a threat. For now, she had a bigger, much more dangerous foe to deal with.

"Power goes both ways, Lucas." She groaned as a tremble of pain washed over her.

"What are you babbling about?" He took a step forward but paused, frowning. "What have you done?"

"Nothing yet." She closed her eyes and held out a hand. "Return what was lost. Put back death. From ashes you were raised to ash you shall return."

"You don't have enough power to harm me." Lucas grinned. "You used it all to destroy your sister."

"Try me." She straightened, willing him to call her bluff. Pushing aside her fear that he would discover her trick too soon and kill her before she could finish this.

"You're nothing without your men," he sneered. "A pathetic witch who'll always be second best."

"That's where you're so wrong. I'm so much more." Using

the last of her strength, she lunged for the blanket, palming the blade in her hand. Her blood still coated the tip. The magic still throbbed in the drops that had soaked the blade of a mother in search of her child. A mother's love and desperation--how even in nature--a mother was a formidable foe.

Lucas teleported in front of her and she jumped back. Fear shooting into her gut.

"Time for your son and you to die!"

Her scream tore through her soul as she held on to the stuffed animal hidden inside the blanket.

He jerked her bundle from her, holding it out of her reach. Then he glanced from her down to the blanket with a confused look. His smile shifted into a frown. He tore the covering off but before he could counter, Asi slammed her dagger into his kidney.

"Join my sister in death, you fucking bastard."

"H-How?" He choked out falling to his knees. "How are you stronger than before?"

She leaned down and whispered in his ear, "I'm a mother now and I will fight you with every atom of my being to protect my family. No one will touch my son as long as I'm alive!"

Twisting the blade, she yanked it out. Lucas gasped, falling onto his side.

Demons around them paused in their fighting, gaping at her. Lucas' body smoldered until there was nothing left but a pile of burnt bones that she crushed under her boot.

"Remind me never to make you mad," the demon beside her who had offered to save Tarrin smirked.

"Why did you help us?" she asked. Sure there were a few demons fighting against their own kind but the easier path would have been to give into her sister and Lucas.

"Unlike some, I believe in love." He glanced behind her,

his dark eyes shining, to Kevin. "And you all have it in spades."

She let out a breath. "Thanks."

"Q." He bowed slightly.

"Just Q?"

"Long story." He stepped aside as Ralph, Simon, Ben and Kevin hugged her at once. The magic holding them had faded away with Lucas and Tara's defeat.

"You did it!" Simon cheered.

"Let's get the hell out of here." Ralph closed his eyes, teleporting them home.

Asi untangled herself from her husbands. "Sorry, I'll rejoice with you all soon. I've got a baby to take care of."

An hour later, Tarrin was cleaned, feed, and sleeping softly on Ralph's chest. Morning light shone through the window. Both Simon and Ben were in their morning comas but she wasn't the least bit sleepy.

"Can we talk?" Kevin asked, his voice soft.

"Sure." She took his hand and led him into their bedroom and closed the door.

Kevin looked like he was going to be sick. His skin had a greenish tone and he couldn't meet her gaze. Why was he so worried? They'd won. Tarrin was back, safe and sound.

"I have a confession." He sat down on the bed, staring at his shoes.

With a heaviness pressing on her heart, she sat beside him, holding his hand in hers. "Whatever it is, I will listen."

"You know I love you, but—" he swallowed and her heart stopped.

Did he not want to be married anymore? Had he fallen out of love with her? Inside, her heart beat frantically. "Please, just tell me."

"I love you, but I need more."

She stiffened. "Like another woman?"

"No," he chuckled, bringing her hand up to kiss her knuckles. "You are all the woman I need. But…Asi…I'm bi. Sometimes I need that part of me. It's a need I tried to hide, tried to strangle. But life is too short."

"Are you in love with one of the others?" Had they been doing this behind her back? She pushed aside her hurt, focusing on Kevin.

"No, none of them. I love you. I love the way you feel when I'm inside you. How your body models with mine. But sometimes I long for something more. Please understand."

"I'm trying to. So what are you wanting?" Her throat felt raw, the words stinging.

"I'm asking if I can bring someone else into our marriage."

She let out a breath. "Kevin, I don't think I can handle any more lovers."

"No," he shook his head, "He wouldn't touch you unless you asked."

"So he and you would have a relationship outside of ours?" She frowned not knowing if she was okay with this or not.

"Yes, but I would tell you before I did anything."

"If you're asking for my permission, don't." She squeezed his hand. "I might not understand or agree with your decision but I won't cage you. Nor will I condone your choices. Hell, we have an unusual marriage as it is."

He offered her a smile. "You're not mad?"

"No." She sighed. Her fears subsiding some now that she had her son and her men safe. "But I wish you'd have talked to me sooner about this. No more secrets, okay?"

"Promise." He kissed her mouth lightly.

"When do I meet the mystery guy?" Her curiosity peeking.

"You already have," Q said as he leaned against the dresser.

She shook her head, too much had gone one for her to readily accept a new member so soon. "I need time for all of this to sink in."

KEVIN - TEN MONTHS LATER

"That's it, you can do it." Kevin held out his arms for Tarrin to walk to him. His son had toddled to each of them during the last several minutes.

Q filmed the first steps on his phone while Asi clapped her hands and laughed.

Kevin never thought he'd find happiness or acceptance. Here, he not only had the love of a wonderful woman but of the other husbands and his own lover, Q even if Asi was still getting used to the idea. Every day she was more and more relaxed around Q. He even caught them whispering about a shoe sale.

"All right, little man, time for your nap." Ralph scooped him up.

Tarrin squealed in delight as they disappeared into Tarrin's bedroom. It was an addition they'd added onto the house originally for Q but the incubus had insisted on staying in Tarrin's old bedroom when he noticed the baby would cry every time he entered the space.

In thanks, Asi had blessed and cleansed the room for Q.

She and he becoming fast friends and their friendship warmed Kevin's heart.

"Say." Q pocketed his phone. "The vamps are asleep, how about you, me, Ralphie and Asi have a little fun together?"

Desire spiked in his groin at images conjured by his lover's words. "How so?"

"Let me show you." Q looked toward Asi and asked, "Sweetie, you in?"

Her cheeks flushed but she nodded. Just thinking about this made Kevin's dick tent his sweatpants. Asi licked her lips, a hunger in her eyes as she glanced between Q and Kevin. Lust spiked and he prayed to god that Ralph would be in on this too. It was new territory having Q in the mix with the others. Excitement and anxiousness twirled in his middle. But the desire to be with them and share this moment and hopefully more, revved up his libido even more.

Asi pushed Kevin down into the recliner, then knelt before him, palming his erection. Q pulled the footrest out so that Kevin reclined all the way back, with Asi climbing on top to reach him. Q leaned over from the top and kissed him allowing his power as incubus to heighten the lust already growing between them.

Kevin gasped, the feeling intense as both of his lovers touched him.

"Fuck!" Ralph entered the living room but his voice held curiosity, not anger.

Asi rose and Ralph spun her toward him. He kissed her, groping her ass, while Q moved from Kevin's mouth to his pants, easing the fabric off him. Kevin's cock springing straight up.

Kevin's yearning flared as Ralph undressed Asi. Q's mouth lowering on Kevin's cock, swirling his tongue along the tip and Kevin gripped both the sides of the recliner. Ecstasy heating his veins.

His body buzzed with desire. "Fuck!"

Q pulled back, smirking. "Your turn, love."

Asi moved from Ralph to Kevin. Her mouth lowered onto his cock, sucking hard. Q grasped Kevin's wrist and bit down, drawing in his blood. Unable to stop the waves of euphoria pounding through him, Kevin grasped Asi's hair with his free hand, guiding her mouth lower. Taking him all in.

Kevin met Ralph's gaze. His eyes were full of hunger and raw sex. He'd stripped down and now fingered Asi from behind. Her scent of arousal filling the air.

She moaned, Kevin's dick popping out of her mouth. "God, I want you both inside me."

Not waiting for an answer, she climbed up Kevin's body, planting herself down on his cock up to the hilt. Her pussy squeezing and clenching him, driving him insane. He thrust up harder and faster inside her. Q shot his power through Kevin again taking the heat, the craving, the fucking to heightened pleasures until Kevin thought he'd explode. *Not yet. Not yet.*

"Ralph!" she screamed. "Get in me now! I'm so horny."

Obeying, Ralph moved behind her, cupping her ass. Kevin fingered her nipple until it stood firm and tight, then he moved to the other. His hand moving down to her sex, stroking her. Q bent Kevin's head back, kissing him. He tasted his blood on the incubus' mouth but he didn't care. He wanted more.

Ralph cupped her buttocks, spreading her cheeks wider. Her eyes rolled back, and she moaned when he pushed his cock into her ass. Then sensation almost made Kevin cum. But he kept the reins on his orgasm as he watched Asi squirmed on top of him. Her breaths becoming erratic. Ralph pumped into her deeper and deeper. Her body expanding to take them both in. She leaned back, her tits bouncing as her orgasm screamed out of her.

Q straddled Kevin's face from the side, allowing him to lick and suck the Incubus' cock while Asi shuddered on top of him. And still, Kevin wanted more. He sucked Q harder until the Incubus shouted his climax.

His lust power scorching down Kevin's throat and into his dick. He groaned, pumping Asi harder, faster as the magic's chain effect brought her own orgasm along with Kevin's. Both of them yelling, then growing still. Sweat glistening off their naked bodies. Ralph grunted a few times as his climax whipped through him as well. Asi laid on top of Kevin while Q slid to the floor, a satisfied grin on his face.

Ralph fell back on his knees, panting. "Holy fuck!"

The scent of sex and musk hung in the air as they all caught their breath.

Asi looked up at Kevin, her face pink. "Can we do that again when Ben and Simon wake up?"

"Whenever you desire." Kevin rubbed her back. As crazy as love was, he'd found it in spades and wouldn't change anything for the world.

ABOUT THE AUTHOR

Autumn Gray has always believed in magic and the paranormal. She found her love of reading supernatural stories during middle school library and devoured all of the mythical books she could find.

When she ran out of books to read in high school, she started writing her own.

Autumn lives with her husband, three kids, two cats and a Jack Russell Terrier that thinks its human.

ALSO BY AUTUMN GRAY

One simple boyfriend spell. One ancient book of magic. What could go wrong?

At seventeen, I'm thrown from my normal life into the supernatural world. One moment I'm planning prom and the next I'm on a one-way bus ride to Hollowheaven's Supernatural Academy where I won't be allowed to see my friends or interact with the rest of the world until I control my power.

Whatever.

This place is weird and I can't help feeling that the academy made a mistake. A huge one.

Just do what I'm told and I'll be able to get the hell out of here.

But when a truth or dare party goes too far, I get in over my head.

Who knew that I could conjure ghosts?

Or that they would be so real to me that I find myself falling for them? If the dean finds out I've screwed with magic, I won't be expelled.

Worse.

I'll be forced to stay here until I get my magical shit together. I can't fall in love with guys who aren't even real--or alive. I've got to figure out a way to get them back into the afterlife before I can't walk away from them. Before I can't stand **not** to have them in my life.

One thing I'm learning is that magic is never simple.

Welcome to the first year at Hollowheaven Supernatural Academy, where not only the grounds are haunted. Scroll up and snag your copy today!

www.ingramcontent.com/pod-product-compliance
Ingram Content Group UK Ltd.
Pitfield, Milton Keynes, MK11 3LW, UK
UKHW040010200726
13854UKWH00001B/120